# BABEL
# AND I

CHARLES MORICE was born into a devout Catholic family, but split with his relatives when he eloped to Paris in 1882, and lost his faith. He began writing for the anticlerical *La Nouvelle Revue gauche*, which changed its name to *Lutèce* with his encouragement, and published Verlaine's *Poètes maudits* as well as offering vocal support to the Symbolist Movement before it folded in 1886. He subsequently assisted in the foundation of the *Mercure de France*. He was better known for his essays than his poetry, but his visionary fantasy *Il est resusscité* (1911; tr. as *He is Risen Again*) and the collections *Quincaille* (Albert Mesein, 1914) and *Rideau de pourpre* (1921) are notable.

BRIAN STABLEFORD has been publishing fiction and non-fiction for fifty years. His fiction includes an eighteen-volume series of "tales of the biotech revolution" and a series of half a dozen metaphysical fantasies set in Paris in the 1840s, featuring Edgar Poe's Auguste Dupin. His most recent non-fiction projects are *New Atlantis: A Narrative History of British Scientific Romance* (Wildside Press, 2016) and *The Plurality of Imaginary Worlds: The Evolution of French* roman scientifique (Black Coat Press, 2016); in association with the latter he has translated approximately a hundred and fifty volumes of texts not previously available in English, similarly issued by Black Coat Press.

# CHARLES MORICE

## BABELS, BALLOONS AND INNOCENT EYES

### Short Stories and Poems in Prose

Translated and with an Introduction by
**BRIAN STABLEFORD**

THIS IS A SNUGGLY BOOK

Translation and Introduction Copyright © 2019
by Brian Stableford.
All rights reserved.

ISBN: 978-1-943813-83-4

# CONTENTS

Introduction / *7*

Listen, Listen, See if it's Raining / *13*
Wanderers / *16*
The Last Temple / *30*
To Flee / *41*
Interior Testimony / *45*
The Little Garden / *50*
Truth / *58*
Nabuchodonosor / *66*
On the Floating Canvas . . . / *75*
Narcissus / *78*
And I am the One of Your Souls . . . / *84*
The Silence Subsides . . . / *85*
Have you Lived . . . ? / *87*
Everything Goes Away / *89*
Dedication of a Book of Joy / *92*
In the Forest / *94*
Woman / *97*
The Thought of the Dead / *98*
The Sergeant and Infinity / *102*

The Indicator / *105*
The Square / *107*
Sonnet / *111*
The Society for the Encouragement of Genius / *112*
Out There / *119*
Vision / *121*
Subjects; or, The Only One / *126*
The Flies / *132*
Other Music / *136*
Compliments / *138*
On the Road, at Night / *141*
François-les-Bas / *148*
I Know Them . . . / *156*

# INTRODUCTION

THE STORIES in this collection are taken from *Quincaille* by Charles Morice, first published by Albert Messein in 1914 and reissued in 1919. The original title signifies "scrap metal," and the justification for that symbolic nomenclature was provided by a brief prefatory "Argument" and a slightly more extensive "Epilogue," but I have preferred to appropriate a different image, from the prose poem "As-tu vécu . . . ?"—here translated as "Have You Lived . . . ?"—which echoes distinctive sentiments expressed in a few of the other pieces collected in the volume and translated herein.

Charles Morice (1860-1919), the son of an officer in the army, was born in Saint-Étienne, near Lyon, into a devoutly Catholic family. After leaving the seminary where he was educated until the age of eighteen, he set out to study law, but he fell in love with a young woman of whom his family disapproved, lost his faith, and ran away with her to Paris in 1882. There he embarked on a career as a journalist and began to write for the anticlerical periodical *La Nouvelle Rive Gauche*. Partly under his influence, *La Nouvelle Rive Gauche* changed its name and editorial direction to become *Lutèce*, the first periodical committed to the ideals and objectives of the Symbolist Movement, which was then making its initial headway under the presiding influence of Stéphane Mallarmé. It was in *Lutèce*, under Morice's auspices, that Paul Verlaine published *Les Poètes maudits*, one of the fundamental documents of the Decadent Movement, which was intricately entwined with the Symbolist Movement, and Morice remained one of Verlaine's most ardent champions thereafter.

Morice was at the heart of the Symbolist Movement for the next decade and a half, involving himself in the founding and editing of several other important Symbolist periodicals, including *La Vogue* and the *Mercure de France*. He published a great many essays, some of which were influential in assisting the careers of fellow writers and such artists as Rodin, Pablo Picasso and Paul Gauguin, but only one novel during his lifetime—*Il est ressuscité* (1911; tr. as *He is Risen Again*), about an ironic Second Coming—and his belatedly-collected poetry only filled a single volume. *Quincaille* similarly collected all his published short fiction and prose-poetry, and also preserved a number of unpublished fragments, some of which were probably spinoff from his unfinished novel *L'Esprit seul* [The Mind Alone], which he intended to be his masterpiece. Morice was, however, widely regarded as a key figure in the Movement, becoming its leading theorist after Mallarmé's death.

In an interview conducted by Jean Émile-Bayard and translated into English in 1926, Morice characterized the Movement briefly as follows:

"The Symbolists protested by their works against, on the one hand, the Parnassian Movement, which refined the superfine to the vanishing point and reduced Art to problems of form; and on the other, against Naturalism, which was the intrusion of scientific and democratic blackguardism into literature. They reopened the temple of general ideas, which the Parnassians thought they had closed forever. They moved the human soul again with the tremor of mystery which Berthelot and Zola believed they had abolished." (Bayard, *The Latin Quarter Past and Present*, Fisher-Unwin 1926, p.219).

Morice did not have a happy life. He quit his first love and the daughter born of that relationship in 1887, and lived alone until 1896, when he married a widow, whose daughter from her first marriage, an infant at the time, who subsequently became a writer under the name Marie Jade, launched her own career in 1925 with a *roman à clef* entitled *Le Masque du génie* [The Mask of Genius] that offers a severely uncharitable assessment of him and the marriage. While the marriage lasted, he and his wife and stepdaughter lived in Brussels, where he taught art history at the Nouvelle Université, but he returned to Paris in 1901. He reconverted to Catholicism in the early 1900s, and much of his writing thereafter showed a strong but unorthodox religious influence—as in *Il est ressuscité*, which offers a highly unconventional Messiah. He married again in 1909—in church, this time—but separated from his wife in 1915. He left Paris for the Midi when his health deteriorated, and died in Menton.

The legacy of Morice's various failed relationships and interludes of morose isolation was reflected in a distinctly jaundiced attitude to life and love, very obvious in his prose-poetry and short fiction. His prose poems and short stories frequently blend the lachrymose and the cynical in a distinctive alloy, shaped by his particular Symbolist method and Decadent style, which bring many of his confessional pieces close to a surreal stream-of-consciousness that was somewhat ahead of its time, but his works span a broad and rich spectrum, illustrated by the selections translated herein.

These translations were made from the copy of the 1919 edition of *Quincaille* reproduced on the Bibliothèque Nationale's *gallica* website.

—Brian Stableford

# BABELS, BALLOONS AND INNOCENT EYES

# LISTEN, LISTEN, SEE IF IT'S RAINING

IN a noble and powerful attitude, leaning on his elbow amid cushions, his forehead in his hand, illuminated by the flickering light of a candle, with a book before his eyes—eyes often distracted, which go astray pursuing visions in the curtains, on the walls and in the dark corners of the vast, sad room—is a Young Man. Whether he is one of those whose hour will not sound, or whether the days to come will be his days, know that he does not care, know, oh, be sure, that glory alone tempts him of knowing what *all this* signifies, *all this* that is life and death, memory without appearance and the past, hope without certainty and the future, the mystery of calices, the problem of eyes and the reasoning of the moon.

Now he turns away from the walls, from the dark corners, from the curtains; it is toward the window that he dreams, wide-open to the redoubtable darkness. Beyond, the nightmare of nocturnal confessions tortures everything that is, and everything that is an endless plaint rises, a plaint rises with the incense of slumbers, rises, borne by Hatred and Amour, rises toward the disdainful clouds, and, in passing, bursts in the tranquil and vast, tranquil and sad, room in which, both orientated toward the same Questions, meditating on the anxiety of life, are the Young Man with the passionate pale face and Goethe, in a portrait, the sole luxury in the sad room, a proposed Ideal of conscious serenity.

A plaint rises, and you see: the host of the living, collapsed, weary, with their burden of lies and confessions, trampling underfoot the dream of things; you see: the host of the living, the man with the two great bitter creases that the disappointment of laughter leaves on his dolorous mouth, the woman with infinite eyes because immense desire and immense despair cannot fill them, and the child who is already weeping in the woman's arms; you see: the host of the living, the host of unfortunates identical from age to age. Go on! Hesitate no longer between their plaint and your book, choose both, listen while reading. Their plaint and your book are two echoes, and there is only one voice—distant, oh, distant! Do you say that the errors of the writer, whoever he is, or his tyrannical authority, and the very prestige of his genius, dazzle you, and that you lose yourself in the detours of a language forced crosswise to the Sense of Right? What does it matter, since the Words know, since they are abundant in supernatural suggestions, since they remain in spite of our departures and since they are sincere in spite of our duplicities? Go on! What is said is utterly indifferent *if you can hear*, IF YOU MUST HEAR. And how do you know—the merit of being!—that you are not the man who was elected since time immemorial to hear the unheard response? Do you know? Who can say?

Listen, then, my brother: the meaning of *all this* is in *all this*; but the words have a significance beyond their noise, even beyond silence. Listen and see when the lips move without speaking, when the eyes have darted their last glance. It is the divine smoke that rises from the broken heart, it is the burning rose of hearts washed with tears, it is the cry—oh, listen avidly—it is the cry of the sick in the night.

# WANDERERS

THE BEAUTIFUL dusty and celebrated feet, the feet returned from everything and still *en route*, O Pilgrims! what wonder they awaken in the souls of children and women!

But the seated, on the stone bench, on the sordid, florid threshold of taverns, awaiting the evening soup, while a chorus of grape-pickers intoxicates the air with merry songs—but the seated, suspicious, watch the pilgrims from who knows where, going who knows where, pass by—but the seated frown at the sight of those who are not of the house. And in the eyes of the sedentary old men, the stubborn laborers, in the eyes, in the eyes in which the sun, reflected by the furrow, only mirrors stains, hatred is ignited, accentuated by scorn, aggravated by envy, for the beautiful white and resonant feet that, being light, having the destiny of going, go lightly.

Attractive figures so quickly effaced at the limit of the horizon, figures always *en route*, which one has not yet seen, which one will never see again, those passing shadows leave in the hearts of women and children the regret of stories, of interminable and beautiful stories that will not be told. The eyelids of the little ones flutter, dazzled by the unknown, and the milk dries up in mothers' breasts.

Disquieting figures, too long persistent on the edge of the horizon, too slow to vanish in the rancor of trembling old men: what if tomorrow, the sons, suddenly astonished by the vine and the labor, their gazes vague in the distance and their hands asleep on the plow, were to waste the hour and the sunlight dreaming of the angelus of other bells?

## I. Fires

Sure of its end as of its origin, unknown; haunted by rare, anxious footsteps; appropriate to apparitions; sometimes straightening up, ironic and blue, to see who is coming: the road to that country, here devoid of towns, traverses devastated forests. No leaves on the trees, and yet the night dwells beneath the black branches, multiplied infinitely. No flower, no moss; thick layers of silent sand, like a sea departed centuries ago. The silence of ordinary darkness, always.

But, invisible from the road, fires burn here and there between the wretched trees, the discreet campfires of Bohemians. Taciturn, with economical gestures, strangers and conquerors everywhere, the tellers of virile adventures arrange their faces spangled with sequins in a circle. In heroic and tranquil poses they listen to the Orient dreaming. They see the Three Sacred Crowns whose scintillating shadow surrounds their road and pales the bloody gold of braziers, and their perpetual ecstasy adores those three initial circles of fabulous Asia, their real mother.

Then, all gazes, quickly exchanged and turned away, encounter one another over the youthful slumber of the pale child, belied by their astral and augural race, a prisoner of the strange amour of the woman who watches, immobile, leaning over the soft, closed eyes; and all those gazes, amid the dreams of the occidental child, infiltrate all the way to his soul the splendor of the Three Crowns, surveying that which he can conceive therein without dying.

Until the most ancient of the Elders redresses all the halts with a signal and assembles them on the road again, after having taken a few solitary steps there, and they all go away, like light phantoms, and all of them, disseminated, go far to the West where the Earth ends, passing indolently, their eyelids lowered, before the good inns, in the evening, were the placid people are, forgotten on the stone bench, who consider them suspiciously, fearing for the crops and holding forth for a long time.

## II. The Voice

"All that you can learn, young man, in this land in mourning, all that you do not know, would you like it to be revealed to you by the rays of the sun or the gleams of the moon, the Word of the Prophets or the kisses of my lips? You have only obtained, as yet, the sentiment, devoid of pride, of your solitude in me, amid their hostility. My joys put you to sleep; in the hour when a few of my caresses can complete the revelation in you, my joys will go to sleep, while the evaded gazes of the Very Wise violate your eyelids and throw you back, awake, into my arms.

"From terror and lassitude—innocence and ignorance—your life has become the resigned habit of a vain agony, and I am dying, and I am also dying of only pouring you miserly droplets of the ecstasy of the profound Truth that beats in my breast with the alternating flames of a divine conflagration.

"For I come from the brilliant cradle of the world and the gods, where they are not feared, where souls are as savant as flowers, where the dance of life turns in liberty. But you, your head full of futile thoughts, go in search of the light without knowing how to repose in it, and I am submissive to your trouble.

"Oh, if you only wanted to sit down at the banquet! If you were only able to want, in a dream more durable than you, to sit down at the banquet where the masters of Truth divide it, in accordance with just measures, between the various humanities! Would you not at least be able to glimpse the essence, the unique and the incorruptible, either in the sonorous features of the word that radiates in the pupils where the veridical sunlight has remained, or in the significant lines of pure beauty?"

### III. Majesty

In the ennui, in the glacial torpor of the senescent race that, weary of turning about itself, scarcely leans over now, here and there, and shakes its diminished brow grotesquely, the sublime Annunciatory Bohemia becomes anxious and torpid, and turns its beautiful errant head toward the Fatherland, where the Three Kings await.

It straightens up its beautiful errant head in a final surge of pride, and, leaving the dust of its feet on our thresholds, seeking to rejoin its soul, already in flight, pensively resumes the road through the forest, where the multiplied branches are devoid of leaves and flowers, the road through the devastated forest.

The orator villages see the exiled passing by, and fall silent while it passes, in order to hasten to burst forth immediately thereafter in discordant discourse, during which it draws away toward the blue horizon, and plunges into the ultimate out there, and fades away, a vision vanished in the ultimate out there.

The fires are reborn, accomplices of the night, and the sublime Bohemia, motionless and silent, meditates as to why the gods have endowed the Occident with that incurable imprudence, that blind and deaf ingratitude.

The most ancient of the elders makes a sign, and the wretched trees catch fire joyfully; that which will no longer be, celebrates as a fête the dawn of its own annihilation.

Then the road shudders with ease, for it knows full well that it is the sublime Bohemia that is regaining its sumptuous fatherland.

Errant heads! Errant heads! While singing real songs!

## IV. The Real Songs

### I

—Vibrant spheres of serenity in the ether, scintillating effluvia of the First Action and the eternal Writing of the Word,

—In scolding the semi-ignorant, who are loquacious, the Moon and the Stars organize expertly the essential delays of the revelation,

—And play their games of the blue of the day and the blue of the night, and the intoxicating pallor of the dead, and the terrible redness of brides,

—And take pleasure, the Stars! the Stars! in rhythming our passing!

### II

—When we are under the radiance of the Three Crowns—brothers, sisters—and when the Voice has said to us: "Speak," that is the order,

—We will prostrate ourselves seven times in accordance with the rite—brothers, sisters—when we will be the radiance of the Three Crowns.

—Men will receive our words in hatred—brothers, sisters—but women will love the clarity of our eyes.

—Children will give us their beautiful infantile laughter—brothers, sisters—and women will burn their eyes in our eyes.

—Masters, masters, it is high time to make the world—brothers, sisters—a new largesse of gold, myrrh and new incense.

—For the marvelous eyes of women will be extinguished—brothers, sisters—when we are under the radiance of the Three Crowns:

—When we are under the radiance of the Three Crowns—brothers, sisters—the sons of man will have lost their divine laughter.

## III

—I kill the flowers, every evening, with a gesture, and then my breath blows them away, for them to weep softly colored clouds, over my slumber in the grass.

—In the grass, when the Sun wakes me up, I leave my shadow lying, in which nothing of my detested memory will any longer germinate—and I pass on.

—In order for me to pass on, the rivers, at my voice, separate; in order that I can pass on, the peoples, at my voice, disperse; at my voice, the monuments crumble, in order that I can pass on.

## IV

—No one can say to me: "Come." Their heroes would die of daring it. When I went into the lands where the Sun sets, merely by seeing me measure the shadow of my staff on the plain at sunset, men left me as my only witnesses the pensive birches of the solitudes.

—I only belong to the road, I have no human existence, I am the One who passes by and there is nothing for me but amour and death, grapnels of their own darkness, collaborating and preparing the egg of life for the turbulent approach of annihilation.

—If ever, in the vertigo of an ancient reality, of which I might perhaps have the tempestuous memory, I have feared the adorable bitterness of death and the redoubtable sweetness of amour, it is because it was necessary that the fatalities of my form should be accomplished within me.

—Now, above amour and death, beyond their concert, beyond the fatalities and above the old desires, I, for whom the clouds and temporary landscapes never weary of changing the décor, have made an innumerable retreat into astonishment and into the fear of successive souls, I, Bohemia, laugh at the traps that their beauty would like to extend for me: I do not love, I no longer live, I shall never die.

V

—I am bringing back from the Fatherland, in a mystic vase, the Secret that I could not spread.

—The peoples have been deaf to me and I am not the One that they ought to judge and crucify.

—I am only the Peregrine Eye by which Those who sent me want to See and Know . . .

—Oh! I am going to resume my great dream, dazzled by the Sun and the Stars, in the Fatherland!

## V. The Child

Standing on the road, alone in the nights whose heavy shadows, sometimes semi-defeated and sometimes victorious, resist the fires of the joy of the death of trees: the Child.

He follows with an astonished gaze the abandonment of the mother who adopted him, the good thief, the great beauty with the illuminated brow who sat him on her knees and spoke to him in a whisper.

How slow her steps are, how heavy her steps are, as she draws away! How regretfully she follows those of her tribe! However, they do not do her any violence. She had to leave him on the road, the Child.

They are not hastening either. They go, their beards over their shoulders, sympathizing with the mother, anxious for the Child, but they go on, and will go on forever, because that is destiny and the law.

The Child cannot follow them, any more than they could linger beside him: their mission is accomplished; it is among those of his own blood and his own sun that he will accomplish his.

Will he remember having been their companion and their pupil? Will he be allowed to speak about it? Will he be allowed to remember? Will he be allowed to *live*? He watches his Bohemian mother draw away slowly.

He gazes through his tears at his Bohemian mother who is going away, and then he turns to the west, and his little shadow extends along the road in the dawn that is nascent behind him, his little tremulous shadow.

He calls out, and distant voices respond to him, those which have been seeking him for many days, amazed to see him, alone on the road, his head haloed by fresh gilded light.

Meanwhile, his little elongated shadow trembles on the road, which will soon be lugubriously illuminated by the last fires of the joy of the death of trees, and will soon receive the calm clarity of the new day.

His little shadow on the road trembles toward those who, for many days, have been searching for him, and close to whom his Bohemian mother has left him, on the road, in front of their house.

Toward those who come from the shadow, his little trembling shadow stretches; they too are trembling, not daring to believe that their prayer has been granted, and they only see the halo about his head.

They are full of lassitude, they have grown old while the Child was growing up, the tenderness in their hearts is embittered and it is by means of reproaches that their joy will be expressed.

(Oh, take care, approach prudently, come in silence; is it not the first word that determines the last? And what is there in common between you and him?)

They are going to say: "My son, why have you acted thus with us? Your father and I have been searching for you, much afflicted."

He will not say to them: "Why were you searching for me?" He does not know yet that his little shadow, in stretching toward those shadows, will rejoin them alone, while his light exiles him; and those who were searching for him can only see that light.

The forest exhales a profound sigh and there are consumed trees that slide into ash and fade away; the profound forest throws out a sheaf of flashes and undulates like a curtain with creases of fire.

Then the fire withdraws its flames and slyly pursued its ravages in the thickets, red dots here and there, while the daylight brightens, displayed in the joyful sky.

The Child has taken a step back, toward the Orient, raising a hand that shines, white and pink, in the air, and his father and mother have also taken, at the same instant, a step toward him.

With a solemn gesture that wards off prophesies, the Child raises his little hand, and they do not know whether he is invoking the angels or ordering them to go away, whether he is rejecting the tenderly avid hands that they held out to him . . .

(—*Put hands together.*)

### VI. Oh, let a Child Live . . .

—Little children are strangers
Who come from afar to learn to live?
—Little children are messengers
From the true God, who invite us to follow them!
*Unknown.*

Oh, let a Child Live, remember and speak, messenger of the Light!

The one who will remember will save the world.

All Children, at one moment of their little lives, have had the good fortune to be stolen by Bohemians . . .

(he gazes through his tears at his Bohemian mother, who is drawing away) . . . and then, beneath the eyelids of Children, that nostalgic Oriental fire broods, which frightens parents. All, or almost all, parents strive to extinguish that light, to turn the gaze of Children away from the interior Fatherland . . . (singing its real songs, the Bohemian troop draws away) . . . and with all the force of their mistaken love the parents blow on those eyes and pour darkness into them.

Take care! In his resistance to the shadow, it might be that the enlightened mind will be irritated against his fearful guardians—they would like to rock him, to put him to sleep in the night of their mistaken love—and it might be that the persecuted mind will be exalted, borne outside itself, losing its fecund virtue for having struggled against Love, against mistaken Love. Mistaken love stimulates a devouring conflagration: the forest fills the sky with smoke, and that enormous torch does not enlighten.

Oh, let a Child live! The truth, our truth, is within him; let him seek it within himself, in order that he can enlighten us all.

Jesus, at the age of twelve, was speaking and teaching in the Temple; as he did, our natural and pure essence will confess the truth that is within us, at the moment of the first awakening of the soul, if the elders, those who have acquired the habit of living, do not hasten to blind that soul by throwing the dust of habit into the eyes.

For happiness and for salvation, the unique legitimate law is that everyone should live in accordance with the desire that he bears, as a Child. The grave instant that is necessary, for happiness and salvation, to surpass is the one in which the Society of Men attempts to constrain the Child to live in accordance with their lie and not in accordance with his own truth. An atrocious struggle, but it is brief: the lie cannot prevail over heroism, the just prerogative of the truth.

The Society of Men yields to the Child, if he resists them. That is how great poets and great artists, the true lights of the world, have succeeded in safeguarding their original soul, their divinely human soul of a Child. Why are great poets and great artists so rare? We would all have genius if we knew ourselves, since genius is the expression of difference, and since souls are all different. Why are so many precious differences soon effaced? A brief struggle, but it is atrocious.

Yes, alas, it can be that the persecuted mind is adulterated, either by fury or by assuetude, and the living cease to live without anyone seeing them die, without anyone thinking of weeping over the new entrant to the innumerable old moving sepulchers.

(—*Oh my son, you shall live!*)

Nature obeys, in the accomplishment of each human unity, the great law of recommencements, It is necessary for the newcomer to traverse, in his mother's womb and then on earth, the cycles of animality. The Gospel and the Church mark the date of the advent of the Son of Man; it is when Jesus interrupts his hidden life to *instruct the learned*; it is when our sons and our daughters, nourished by nature, have liberated themselves in order to taste the bread of the Spirit. The learned and all men ought then to incline, listening and full of respect, before the One who knows and who designs to speak.

But the learned argue and all the men reprove. It is necessary to initiate the One who knows in error, to impose silence on the One who designs to speak, and, if he persists in his dangerous folly, he will be outlawed; he will be the savage and the rebel, a social monster, like Jesus and the Poets, like the Bohemians, the Tziganes, the Gitanes and the Zingaris. The man of the truth will be the man of disorder in the torpid world that he has come to wake up. The One who brings the law will have to camp, a "Bohemian"—is that not what they say?—on the other side of their law.

He will be alone everywhere, wandering, dispossessed of all worldly goods, of all the goods of this needy world, which he could redeem with a word, he, the Child—King of the Kingdom of God, of this forgetful world that would like to prevent him remembering, of this lost world that he wants to save, in making himself a messenger of the Orient and the Mages, the new largesse of Gold, Myrrh and the new Incense, of this agonizing world that he wants to resuscitate, pure Child, by illuminating it with the divine light of his simple life, made of all true remembered lives.

(*The One who can remember will save the world.*)

Oh, my son, who was quietly stolen by the good Bohemians, sing us their real songs!

## THE LAST TEMPLE

ON a night of insomnia and autumn a poet was wandering, overwhelmed by thoughts and in their sole company, through immense Paris. The atmosphere was calm. Beyond the heavy sheets of electricity one divined the stars, without seeing them; for we have extended between the sky and ourselves an artificial curtain of blinding darkness, which hides the real light from us.

Paris, that splendor of daylight, that daze, recovers in the peace of nights a veridical beauty. Paris is a liar in the sunlight, with its fake luxury and its vain decoration, with its feverish agitation, which is certainly not the movement of life, with its morbid excitation, with its laughter, which is certainly not that of joy. It becomes true again in the peace of nights.

Then a thousand details, which the diurnal vertigo does not allow us to see, take on in the eyes of the dreamer a profound meaning, often disquieting, often frightening. Night judges day severely and forces it to confess bleak verities.

The poor slender trees of the boulevards, which have I know now what caricaturish dolor, a ridiculous sadness, those pretentious plumes that maintain their alignment and their regimental distances, those exiled plane trees, those sickly chestnuts that never provide any shade and only drink dust, suddenly, when night falls, change their attitude. They were only "planted there," now they straighten up; one might think that they were integrating one another or signaling to one another; one fears that they might be threatening; one might say that they were calling to account the spectacles submitted to them; the silence that envelops them causes consternation.

And the houses are also transformed. Banal enormities in the light, they become, in the obscure hours, massive heaps of revealing shadows, or denouncers of black mystery. Their windows are eyes in which a reflection of the moon is sometimes fixed, with the strange vitreous acuity of a seemingly dying gaze. What! The life that was agitating *there*, still vibrant a little while ago, is now reposing, and it is now death that is looking at us from *there*? Alas, it was not life, it was its parody, and it is not death either. The lie is not interrupted. And I think about "roofs bounded by black sleep"; I picture the acts, I even imagine the dreams of the unknown people *waiting* there.

Of all that gesticulates or lies, consciously or unconsciously, behind the immobile walls, the heavy and captious emanation of secrets falls upon the belated passer-by; that is the meaning of the fixed gleam of windows. They remain incommunicable to whoever truly lives, and like another world; that is the mortuary character of the gleam—and the doors are mouths, firmly shut.

At such hours, the poet, in reckless flight in the tumultuous exile of the streets by day, is careful not to hasten his steps. He does not belong. He is possessed by a poignant curiosity, which frightens him and which he would not want to elude. Something is waiting for him, or about to surge forth, which he does not know: perhaps an explanation. He is ready to hear and to see. The sudden apparition of a realized abstraction, the impossible in a sensible guise, would not astonish him. And that is because the analogical link (in fact, it would reveal everything to us if we knew how to read) by which beings and things are eternally and universally bound together, the intimate, essential relation of the elements of the world, *the unity of life*, imposes itself with an overwhelming evidence at such hours.

The indiscreet brutalities of the great solar din steal those clarities from us—and then, everyone, during the day, observed by everyone, puts on an act for everyone else. Why would one lie by night? For whom? The actors in the drama, now being no more than spectators, listen to the counsel of sincerity that the very décor gives them. The poor courtiers, mad for the frivolity of their furbelows until dusk, now, under the soon-ineluctable wind of menace, go straight to the precise goal, like libertines; like assassins and thieves; like poets: to lucre, stupor, or crime; to Joy; to the liberating truth, personal and eucharistic to all, which radiates after the extinction of the chandelier of the immense theater and the wan footlight of the moon or electricity, those two dead stars, has lit up.

※

Thus a poet went forth, that night.

After five years of absence, five years of studious sojourn in a peaceful neighboring country,[1] he had returned to Paris, the day before, in order to resume, well-armed, his rank in the quotidian battle of letters and life.

And he had been subjected—a double effect of space and time during which progress (is it not?) in the capital had continued—to a sentiment of fear before the multiplied agitation of the great city. That same evening, along the boulevards where the cosmopolitan crowd swirls, considering the sparkling "cafés" and overflowing "terraces" where thousands and millions of living beings sit down at their leisure, forgetful—what philter have they drunk?—of hunger, of malady, of failure and all the innumerable Miseries, he felt suffocated by the irrespirable lie with which contemporary life is supersaturated.

The incarnation, sometimes charming, always murderous, infinite and unique, of that lie, he admired tremulously and detested pityingly in those ambulatory specters that we still call, scornful of the beautiful truth, women, those creatures of prey and joy, those sterile victims of international vice. They symbolize with a cruel evidence our barbarity. They emanate fatally from the present pneumatic void of souls. They are organic syntheses of negations: of Beauty, Amour, and even Lust; they are the dancers of the sacrilegious ballet that, in the endless theater of the street, mocks that Holy Trinity. No more than the genius of being beautiful and the virtue

---

1 Presumably 1896-1901, when Morice was in Brussels.

of loving, do those cold prostitutes possess the art of pleasure.

*Amour, amour is dead with sensuality!*[1]

And in the entirely exterior dream, which begins with their learned smile—but which they nevertheless *never finish*—no thought shines; however, it is the most spiritual essence, for they only exist to offer a mirror to our artificial destinies, a sincere mirror in which the fire without brightness burns of our artifice and our decadence. All that remains of the true in the civilized modern man—the animal—shivers at the revelation of that supreme, abominable truth. O those icy mirrors, those flameless kisses! For how many is Amour not that? Such as they are, these whores, these chastised victims, still fulfill the most august employment, and that is why everything tends toward them—who go forth aimlessly—from the parasitic displays of the big stores into which entry (and exit) is free, where the disorderly forms and colors and all the unjustifiable caprices of a trivial society are conceived in accordance with views to basely and so clearly harmonic, so unique and, one must believe, so appropriate to communal desire that they find their expression in an acceptance, arbitrarily exclusive but universally understood, and—a word once rare but fallen into current usage—*suggestive* of those other counters, those of food and drink, where the beast goes to refuel.

---

[1] Author's reference: "Leconte de Lisle." The line is from "L'Anathème" in *Poèmes barbares* (1872).

※

Night counted its hours. The boulevards were gradually depopulated.

Are those prostitutes, the poet thought, really going about aimlessly? Is life, in their wake, devoid of orientation? Or, let's see, what else is there? Strangers to amour, to sensuality, they are machines for constant, instantaneous, impersonal enjoyment. That is how they meet the needs of my contemporaries, the host of my humble contemporaries, those who regularly or occasionally work in order to live; it is them that I care about, by night, the street not inviting me to remember the rich. My contemporaries have no other future than the moment in the process of passing—the incessantly walking streetwalker is that passing moment—and no other ideal than material wellbeing, immediate and unshared, for material wellbeing only solicits egotistical appetites; my glass and my clothes can only belong to me, and a society in which every member has immediate enjoyment for an objective only makes them enemies of one another.

No union, therefore; the dispersal is dissimulated in the confusion. No collective consciousness; but everyone wants to oblige everyone else to think like him. No communal endeavor; individual effort toward the possession of the instruments of enjoyment. To that effort we deliver ourselves in the shadow, the color of which we carry on us in order "not to stand out." If some, those who possess, associate, it is in a complicity of tyranny, and to defend themselves against those who do not yet possess. And that complicity is disguised in Law, in Morality and in Religion, which are the lies of proprietors. And if, against that complicity, others cry: "Liberty! Equality!" they are the lies of the proletariat. And if the lies from below, more poignant, being full of tears, appear more excusable, they are no less egotistical than the calculated, pot-bellied lies from above. The square-dance of the rich and the poor changes nothing, fundamentally. The sterile foundation of things, nowadays, is the desire for immediate enjoyment. That desire engenders the two series of lies, on the instability of which society is founded—the "civilization" and "progress" of modern life.

But it is *uninhabitable*, that life dedicated to hatred! It is unbreathable! Those beings that are swarming in all directions, gnawing the earth, no more resemble true human beings than malady resembles health, folly resembles wisdom or vice resembles amour. And, in fact, I think there once was a Humanity. It strove to install in immense life the reign of the sensible mind. There was once, at brief and sublime moments of history, a magnificent humanity. Admirable vestiges of it remain, from which life has withdrawn. What, then, has done the work of death? What has killed humanity?

It is evident that industry, the vainglorious daughter of arrogant science, lavishes egotism with means of satisfaction. Is it necessary to accuse industry? Science? Edison? Berthelot? Why has lightning been put in the hands of idiots? Why incessantly turn the living away from the problem of their destiny with new "distractions"? Nowadays, their great affair is eluding distance and cheating time. As for the problem of good and evil, that does not concern us yet. Morality will be the conquest of an omniscient humanity, the crowning achievement of the whole scientific edifice.

In the meantime?

In the meantime, there is night! It is irrespirable, the mephitic modern night, ripped like a storm-cloud by the electric lightning that underlines, designs and renders the darkness sensible without dissipating it. And we agitate, here and there, in the night—some, the best, in crying out to the dawn like lost children and offering ourselves to all sacrifices; others, the majority, in dragging ourselves around, groping in pursuit of vain forms that promise us pleasure, and meditating on all forms of violence. And our "masters" boast of having prolonged the average duration of such a life! And they demand our gratitude for that achievement! But we respond to that: You have lied to us. The life to which you are condemning us is inhuman. Where, then, in the city in which we are imprisoned, thanks to you, have you built the Temple of Hope? Where have you at least erected the white stature?

And the poet evoked the horrible, perpetual every-man-for-himself of a modern street, the dismal tumult of silent people in the racket of things: where are they going? In their instinctive desire to flee a negative and monstrous life, where are they going? And as if he had hoped to see, in fact, the refuge for which everyone was searching in vain, the poet looked around, and suddenly had an illumination.

He was in the spacious crossroads where the three boulevards Saint-Denis, Sébastopol and Strasbourg meet, the first separating the other two from one another.

The profound meaning of modern humanity is written there in stone: there is the Last Temple—oh, not that of Hope!

Yes, a temple! A considerable Gothic church, so vast that it wanted the sky for a vault. Three naves: the central, the continuation of the boulevards Sébastopol and Strasbourg; the lateral the Rue and the Faubourg Saint-Denis to the left, the Rue and the Faubourg Saint-Martin to the right. And in order to make more precise the architectural sense of naves, those two rood-screens, the old Portes Saint-Denis and Saint-Martin, majestic hieroglyphs inscribed there by history in order that the poet might decipher them some day.

Three naves, with the Place du Châtelet for a parvis. It even seems, by virtue of a colossal derision, that its builders did not want to neglect the baptistry, proportionate and appropriate: the Fountain of the Sphinxes.

But what God is adored in this temple?

Open your eyes. Look at the edges of the naves, those shop windows, which certainly have nothing mystical about them. Nor is there anything mystical in the two theaters of the parvis, nor in those distributed along the central nave. The ancient legends have been destroyed, abolished. A new God is served here. So, two churches of a religion of old, have been rejected, to the right and the left going toward the choir, two churches devoid of beauty, which defended the past poorly against the jealous present, and which, dispossessed of all privilege, had already been subjected to the leveling of alignment.

The choir? What choir?

Open your eyes, look in front of you: *the Railway Station.*

The incontestable sanctuary of the Last Temple.

The rites there are categorical and harsh; the anthems and the canticles devoid of grace or tenderness. The cassolettes smoking there do not have the odor of incense. However, as in the other religions, you find in this one an interpretation of the mysteries of death and amour. It is a place of commencement and termination, that temple. It is the fatherland of tears and kisses of farewell. But—a frightfully audacious denial of divine hopes—two idols reign there exclusive of any other worship: Time and Money. The sound of gold tripping over the copper of ticket-windows, the cry of the minutes, that tearing screech that locomotives exhale with the stinking smoke, those are the rites of the Last Temple.

And it seemed to the poet that everything was now clarified for him. The mad agitation of great cities was explained to him. Where are people going in such great haste? They are not *going*, they are going *away*—going away from everything! *Quickly!* And thanks to science, thanks to industry, going *ever more quickly!*—and ever more vainly, for the rapidity of communications between various points in space suppresses, along with distances, differences. Soon, Paris and Peking will be cities similar to one another and to New York, and it will be perfectly stupid to change places, since nothing will any longer tempt curiosity in a world identical everywhere, and since commercial transactions can be carried out from afar.

People will, however, continue to displace themselves, the goal of modern life being precisely and uniquely to change location. Quickly! Ever more quickly! In pursuit of the passing moment! To the station!

   Now, the station itself is only a vague point, a place of temporary destination where a hundred tracks intersect, each one leading to another station. Quickly, ever more quickly, crushing the living, or, as on the boulevard that covers the Saint-Laurent cemetery, trampling over the dead, to go no matter where, to flee other human beings, to flee oneself!

The poet read with a bitter joy in the book of the night those confessions of the city. He agreed that the Religion of Sterile Movement must inevitably be that of the human being dedicated to the perpetual quest for immediate enjoyment; recoiling fearfully from the edge of his own thought, the human being who has condemned himself, logically, to going around the world, perpetually and pointlessly. He has lost the veritable sense of life and is similar to those pitiful streetwalkers, devoid of beauty and devoid of amour, who go on, and on . . . Like them he goes on, lips creased in a stupid smile, in the vertigo of the void of his soul, in the scorn of everything that was his glory, he goes straight ahead, he goes away from himself, defaming his past, insulting nature, and spreading in his passage the odor of his own decomposition . . .

   A beautiful autumnal morning was beginning to quiver, radiantly, and the divine light, the light that creates belief and will, which creates love, submerged the naves of the Last Temple with its splendors.

## TO FLEE

TO flee. To flee along the roads and river banks, and see people, scattered here and there, to rediscover, in the novelty of faces, in the unfamiliarity of landscapes, and to meet up at the terminus, in the conclusive apotheosis of all efforts, in the justified holocaust of glory, epiphany! and in the seductive nudity of one's own truth, O Don Juan of oneself!

Reading—and readings! And, the squandering of the soul, speech! Conferences in the evening and nights, on the rims of glasses, or in accordance with the perpetual boulevards, as circular as the arabesque of speculations—with the dolorously stupid episode of the espalier smile of sad sisters at the passage of the chatterbox, also attained by the frightful desire to sell her beauty.

Oh, heavy, the horizon of the light City where the terror, influenced by the dolor of no longer being itself, already threatens to renounce the becoming! A regret is mingled there for the hero that one might have been, once—once!—whatever people say. But that which they believe one is, one is, if one consents to be, for the sake of indulgence and to excuse them. (And malevolent intoxication leans the elbows of its laughter on the marble, which suddenly seems that of a tomb, and the pitying kiss trembles on adored lips, where sadness curves and closes the ascendant wings of the smile.)

To others, as to me, Paris was the bitter fatherland of obstinate and sterile recommencements. Others remained there stubbornly, fond of their illness. Who knows whether, via the turnings of the great roads, they had not reentered as masters the home of the evil stepmother? I shall attempt the great roads. It did not lie to me, the October dawn in which I heard the appeal of the Orient so clearly. I shall attempt the great roads. In the changing margins of the indefinite I shall go in quest of the renewal of the décor, and I shall interrogate people in passing as to the Desirable Conditions.

I shall attempt the great roads.

. . . I would like to arrive, one autumnal and northerly evening, in some enormous city, new for me, alone and without method, to wander until daylight, with the sentiment of being lost in my solitude and amid the indifference of aspects, without the hope of a refuge in which to resume the familiar life of my thoughts. Perhaps, from that distress, after the ordeal, thanks to the effort, another or a final Self would be born.

Yes, in some heavy metropolis of coal and mist, from recent luxury denounced by the remains of an old style, from labor swarming around scarce aristocratic idleness, in some miserable city proud of bearing the burden of centuries on the monumental front of its barracks, its palaces, its prisons, its churches and its banks—yes, there . . .

All the streets are similar; what I have not seen yet, I shall see again: men and women hurrying, in a hurry—and I am one of them—without knowing where they are going; sometimes a house with a door ajar, projects a gleam, a plaint, and then goes out, falls silent, and the interminable street extends its desolate line, gray beneath the gray of the sky; there would be nothing to see if, written in a universal language with the phosphorescent sweat of the day, words of hatred and fatigue, lust, avarice and vanity were not set out before me by the walls . . .

Yes, there, alone, nameless among the anonymous, soiling myself with "the City," with its ugliness and its beauty, its atrocity and its grandeur, and, stripped and delivered of old ideals, to die, in everything that comes from it to die in me, to be reborn outside it—or to be Born!

And then, I would like, at the bend of a river, on the edge of a plain, with infancy, one summer, until the approach of ennui, to savor repose; to merit the confidence of animals, to enter into the life of things; to devote an hour to the possibility of being a drop of water, a drop of pure water in which the infinite sky admires itself. I would soon have forgotten, as you can imagine, the lumber of written centuries. Oh, I wouldn't be interested in anything, anything at all—except the divine play of light and shadow on the clouds and on the summits, on the plain and on the river; sometimes, closing my eyes, I would rediscover that play of colored elements in the bleating of flocks and the calling of pastors, and in the blue song of bells, the somber blue song of nearby bells, which brightens as it draws away—in the somber blue and gradually brightening blue and soon almost white in which the sobs of orphans and the cry of virgins, the horns of hunters, the laughter and tears of cradles and the verbiage of old men vibrate.

Yes, I would like, Mother, Mother, your child whom you misunderstand, at the summit of my summer, to contemplate you and understand you, and to go to bed, reconquered, on your breast—in order to simplify my soul to your rhythm, and purify it, that it might be worthy of us, O Nature and my Dream!

Then, armed with love and serenity, dreaming of maternal Nature, I would traverse cities and landscapes, and the immense detail of Life, with new eyes, which would see. And the interior drama would become conscious of itself in the décor, as thought would be amplified in the experience, varied along the great roads, of all the universal solidarities . . .

# INTERIOR TESTIMONY

## I

THE GENTLE line of the plains undulates in the distance of eyes and attenuates in the neat darkness, beyond the empire that the Moon holds, and no path is indicated across the labored terrains where I go, wearied by the journey, already long, and wearied further by the difficult march over the slippery ground, which seems to flee beneath my steps. But however far I go, without the certainty of attaining it, toward a goal capable of luring me, I go valiantly, proud of going.

## II

For days and days I have been marching thus, and the gentle ironic line of the plains has not ceased undulating to infinity. The Moon and the Sun have risen by turns and set in the sky of this landscape that astonishes my courage or my candor, and I sense clearly that I am going along an endless road. But I have measured my eternity against its own; they are equal.

## III

Something like a habitual intoxication has gripped me, although it appears that I am not alone. An invisible multitude surrounds me: my Dead. I converse familiarly with them; I will say more, I argue; for we are not in accord, and gladly, if you find us a judge—very gladly—I will ask him to arbitrate between them and me. Nevertheless, even if it makes me seem litigious, I would consent even more to reckon with them—if only I could!

## IV

They say that I am wrong to follow this route after them, for they have followed it in vain, and that I will not see the end of it any more than they did. They say that to the left and right, on the banks of cool springs, on the slopes of florid hills, in the hollows of soft valleys, in the depths of clumps of hawthorn, delights are in preparation, banquets set up, women without veils recumbent, and children singing, without understanding them, odes in which Amour is celebrated. They say . . . and the gentle line of the plains undulates in the distance of the eyes.

## V

"O my elders, my Dead, my very dear, all these benefits, all these benefits with which you solicit me, more than any other I have savored them, more than other I have bathed all my senses in the sweet horrors of all sensualities. But one morning, the morning of a feast day, the young Roman Sextius, his head still crowned with festival roses, saw passing, borne by four holy women, in her open coffin, the Christian woman Sextia, who had just died for having confessed her faith . . ."

## VI

They interrupted me with loud cries, in which I perceived: "Some for the sake of melancholy devotions like yours, others for the sake of ambitious hopes, and others because they were Scholars, and others because they were Poets, all your dead—as disobedient as tearful—have wasted their lives running after chimeras. Oh, you will hear them forbid you, their heir, to imitate their folly and their misfortune, you, the last stake of revenge against Destiny . . . !" They spoke—and the gentle ironic line of the plains has not finished undulating to infinity.

## VII

"My very venerated Dead, since the young Roman Sextius has seen the beautiful face of the defunct Sextia, the

Christian woman, the liquor of Cyprus has lost its savor for him and the vital colors on the most beautiful faces irritate him and sicken his heart. The taste of Life has become insipid for him since he has suspected the taste of Death . . ." (Then the multitude that surrounds me makes a terrible gesture of silent anathema.)

## VIII

"O my Dead! The living eyes of the skeptic Sextius adored the splendor of the faith that he saw radiant in a flash of features forever asleep and rigid. What he felt he could not say, and questions only awakened from his dream, to the peril of his questioners. But it is not the contagion of belief that he desires, nor the contagion of dying. It is the impossible that he is attempting, it is to see through closed eyes, it is to believe by means of a heart that is no longer beating . . ."

## IX

For, young as he is, the Roman Sextius has lived too much to be able to believe and to be able to die. However, since Death and Faith have loomed up on his route, he remains uniquely avid for the spectacle that magnifies humanity to the extent of God—and all day, every day, he follows in dream the Appian Way where he once encountered the cortege of the defunct Sextia, and those who see him pass by talk among themselves in low voices.

## X

With words bathed in tears, my dear and very compassionate dead sympathize with my wretched mania, and, in order to console them, I say to them: "O my elders, my Dead, my very dear, the dream of the Roman Sextius is not my dream, but like him, before he encountered the dead Sextia, I have drunk from the cup of follies to which your wisdom invites me, and like him, I have now lost my taste for Bacchus and Venus. No pale virgin has, however, arisen in my passage and I have not seen the cold eyes of the stone Sphinx that guards your tombs weeping. But, innocent or guilty, I want a spectacle that merits my contemplating it; it is toward that spectacle that I have set my route, and it is before it that I shall stop. O my masters, it is your fault, in sum, if I am immortally unsatisfied; why have you not realized that which would crown and seal my pride in being human? I am sad and disgusted with the forms in which you have, with predilection, reflected your finite forms—and I am going, I am going, I am going still, toward the ultimate Out There, toward which the gentle, ironic line of the plains draws me."

# THE LITTLE GARDEN

Memory is a place full of tears.
Ernest Hello.[1]

CONFIDENTIAL preserve of memories, none mock you publicly, of whom you constitute the regal secret, in hours of solitude, in hours of the soul. It is ordinarily with the second dusk that they arrive, between twilight and darkness; something trivial, or less, evokes them, and I know eyes a long time reproved of tears that a phrase from a hurdy-gurdy has suddenly drowned, because of indistinct connections between a note, perhaps a croak, of the plaintive instrument and some voice. The evocations of vision are as powerful as those of hearing, but in that genre, the great panoramas of the sea, the plain, the mountain or the city do not have—and how necessary it is!—the virtue of a corner of grass and trees devoid of beauty, comparable at close range or at a distance to any

---

[1] Ernest Hello (1828-1885) was a Catholic apologist who published a volume of proto-Symbolist fiction, *Contes extraordinaires* (1879) as an appendix to his numerous theological and philosophical tracts.

other of trees and grass into which the wind of life has thrown us . . .

※

The rickety door to the little garden was as *we* had left it. Now, as then, the naïve judas hole yawned its sad gap, through which our gazes once mingled. The threshold crossed, the desolate spectacle of that courtyard, still green and florid in my memory, delighted my heart with a delectable melancholy, the delight of a true melancholy, of a melancholy for me alone, without witnesses; one of those sincere melancholies such as one does not see, since to allow a melancholy to be seen is to lose its sincerity.

I do not know how many seconds, appreciable seconds, I stood immobile in order to savor my intimate mourning at leisure; then, through the indulgent trellis of leafless branches, I examined the house—and my memory was already scrutinizing the rooms. But I had the scruple of a sort of indiscretion, the fear of something akin to an imprudence. Are they not right, the Sages who say to us: *Do not march any longer in the paths of yesteryear, do not reopen the books of old?* The trees chilled by the autumn wind, murmured: "The ashes of spring have not retained flames"—and I knew that it would have been delicate to close the tottering door again and go away at a slow pace, my head slightly bowed, my hands swinging congruently, content in the end to imagine what I might have seen if I had looked . . .

Curiosity prevailed.

In the deserted garden I caused the old dead leaves to cry out beneath my feet pitilessly, observing in passing the irremediable ruination of the rare flowers that we had planted ourselves. The sweet hour had not lasted long! I climbed the steps of the balcony whose unsealed stones trembled, and I went into the vestibule.

Deserted the garden, deserted the house.

And what a lovely sentimental despair I promised myself!

What? Am I going to lie about my impressions? It is, alas, only too true to say that they were false. I hoped to weep. I was bored. The insipid odor, the soiled, torn papers, the bare rooms, the tarnished windows . . . Only the mirrors tried to move me a little. Also tarnished, they reflected me regretfully. And I thought I was dreaming: they remembered! It was as if they had died of fidelity, and were reproaching me, for my infidel memory, for bringing into the one-time nest a memory disabled by time, deodorized of the already old glory of my joys, a demi-blasé romantic sensibility, only spurred by a desire for further peripeties. And in those mirrors, full of the dust of my forgetfulness, in that décor as faded as my youth, I was, in my own eyes, only the grimacing caricature of my good times . . .

Very appropriately, a sound of footsteps in the garden awoke me from my humiliating reverie. But, without any urgency, expecting the surly face of some indolent gardener, I looked out of a widow—and what was my surprise!

A large black hat shaded the face, but the stride was youthful, the costume elegant and somber. She stopped in the middle of the garden, slowly looked around her, slowly and meticulously, and then, her hands well gloved with mourning, took from her little sleeve a handkerchief edged in black, which she pressed to her eyes.

Within me, astonishment quickly ceded the empire of my soul to an intense, burning jealousy. Oh, the legend of the damned soul who senses, fleeing beneath his fingers without moistening them, the malevolent water of the Cocytus! Such, for me, were those tears.

Who that stranger was, and of what she had come in search, my jealousy denounced to me more surely than any speech could have done. That woman was my victorious rival. She too had been tempted by the paths of yesteryear, but she had not had to take many steps in order to recognize there, living an eternal life, the dazzling specter of former happiness. And I . . .

Politeness and kindness counseled me to silence, and even not to allow myself to be seen, but rather to hide. But I could not resist manifesting my presence somehow, as a vengeance; I coughed.

She raised her head; she perceived me.

A long face, pale and beautiful, with the singularity of large, very dark eyes, inclined toward the temples in the Chinese fashion; the corners of the mouth were almost convulsively lowered.

How I regretted having yielded to the impulsion of mediocre sentiments! The harm was done, and, difficult as my role was, it was at least necessary to keep to it. I bowed, with an emphatic hint of respectful sympathy.

The lady was so perfectly bewildered that she forgot to turn her head away—but could I, however, eternalize my discreet salutations? I took advantage of a sudden step back that she finally took to implore her, with a fervent gesture, to stay there and wait for me, and I went down into the garden.

And as if I believed that I were talking to the owner of the place, I explained that I was a stranger in the house but that I had *lived in it once*, and I begged her to excuse my presence. The lady seemed embarrassed; then, after a silence, said that she herself "had no right . . . had entered at hazard, having found the door open . . . thinking that the house was empty . . . that she too had *lived in it once* . . ." She pronounced that last phrase in a broken voice that moved me.

"Perhaps," I hazarded to say, "we were both brought here by the same motive."

She looked at me anxiously.

"Perhaps it's the past that we're both seeking in this debris."

She shivered and blushed, as if ashamed to have been divined, and took a step backwards. But her heel collided with a stone, and I only just had time to prevent the most lamentable of falls. She avoided, with a smile, the annoyance of thanking me, and, as if the little accident had brought us together, she said: "Yes, and doubtless there's more than one person for whom the things of the past limit the horizon of the future. Memory is their only hope."

That was said in a precise voice, in a soft tone, and her eyes, still luminous with tears, accompanied the dolorous thought with a beautiful gaze.

"Forgive me for having troubled you," I said, taking a step toward the door.

"But . . . I could make you the same apology, and . . . why are we embarrassing one another? Without being yours, my memories are sympathetic to them in advance."

I had desired, without hoping for it, that permission to stay. She took, from my unexpected company, a meaning quite specious for me, and I felt profoundly grateful to her for having come to give such intensity to my vague dolor. My egotism was displaced. With her bizarre features, in which something prematurely worn out attracted my sympathy, the stranger became the very soul of my own sentiments, which had found a poignant freshness in her genuine sadness.

"However," she continued, "as you please; your pilgrimage"—she smiled in order to palliate the ambitious term—"is finished, mine beginning."

"Madame," I said, a trifle solemnly, "I believe that you are one of those whose presence has never been manifest without being essential, and, I divine, you were lacking to my sincerity."

She looked at me for a moment, seeking, not to understand me, but to assure herself that I really understood myself the import of my words. I met her gaze, and discerned there the gradual, hesitant birth of an intention not to be interpreted correctly. And that interior combat was accompanied by an expression of the entire physiognomy, grave and dignified, which forbade any mistake.

Finally, the assurance was established, and with an easy, gracious, noble gesture, the stranger took my arm.

I bowed slightly. At a measured pace we completed traversing the garden together. Then we climbed the steps of the little perron and the pilgrimage, therefore, commenced.

We did not speak. I must have perceived very quickly that I had disappeared from the preoccupations of my companions. Nothing was reflected in her face but defunct realities, and, visibly, in the mirrors that had seemed tarnished to me, in the obscure corridors where I had not been able to see anything—everywhere, in sum— she rediscovered an adored shadow, as living and varied as life. Oh, certainly, she had truly lived, that woman, she had loved! Beautiful and touching, a choice soul and heart, she retained, of the happiness fled, the gratitude of a sensibility, of which death or absence had not interrupted the vibration . . .

We went back down into the garden, and I sensed that there, my presence, effaced in the house, resumed its rights. Strangely, I was embarrassed. The moment of separation came and, without afflicting me, it troubled me; all personal thought had quit me; I was only thinking of giving *forever* a worthy meaning to that rare being and the unique hour. I would have liked to encounter a gaze to which mine could have said, in a flash, everything that betrays the long arabesque of words—but the visitor's eyes were lowered now. Where was her soul wandering?

"Madame," I said, softly, in order that she would look up at me—but her eyes, still full of the past were like the mirrors of the old house—"I shall not forget this late afternoon; it is a memory added to all those that are dormant here for me, and will henceforth lie here in a dreamless sleep, for I am seeing this place for the last time."

Her eyes had brightened, and her attention stimulated. A shadow of sadness passed through them, and—at least I thought so—they interrogated me.

"I shall never come back."

O sincerities of hazard! I said those harsh words with an inflexion of tenderness in which my memories were mingled with an almost amorous admiration for her, which it would have seemed sacrilegious to me to want to reveal.

And, with a salutation full of regrets, as we had arrived on the threshold of the little garden, we quit one another—unknown.

# TRUTH

*That which must not be said.*

IT was a Friday the thirteenth, at a quarter to five in the morning, in a kingdom that I shall not name, that She sprang from her well, stark naked, as everyone knows.

The chamberlain, Rigobert, who was passing by—excuse the belated hour; he was a little fatigued, because of Bacchus and Venus—perceived the creature and thought he was dreaming. But, the vision persisting, he believed his eyes and opened his arms wide.

"Oh, Madame, Madame!" he cried. "Have you no shame? At least think that the night is cold . . ."

He spoke while running; when he was three paces away from her he stopped short.

Standing in the dawn, and even paler, serenely, Truth looked at him without really seeing him; her arrogant bosom of a young warrior defied the wind and her small and muscular feet took possession of the earth, The fellow had never seen so much beauty, and he remained open-mouthed and trembling, waiting for Truth to open her cold and serious mouth.

As, however, she seemed little inclined to loquacity, the old libertine recovered his assurance and chaffed: "Seriously, beautiful lady, this won't do, and I imagine that you're not from around here! Let me spare you a cold or the lock-up."

So saying, he threw over the radiant shoulders his ridiculous and sumptuous mantle of a dignitary of the court.

She let him do it, her thoughts elsewhere; and it was comical and saddening to see Truth decked out in the baubles of human vanity.

"Where are you going?" he asked.

She looked at him without responding, but now she *saw* him, and, under the mysterious action of that gaze, he felt something unknown to himself quivering in his breast: his soul! His soul, which had just been born, ill at ease in its senile prison.

Suddenly, falling to his knees, he murmured like a prayer:

"O divine Beauty!"

She looked at him even more fixedly.

"From where to do know me?" she asked.

(It is necessary to know that Beauty is the nickname of Truth, the amorous name that the gods give her.)

He shivered without comprehending.

She took him by the hand. "Guide me."

Rigobert set forth, for the order was given in a tone that brooked no reply; but the poor chamberlain was rather embarrassed: guide her where?

He did not think for an instant of taking her home. Not that he was worried about the scene that Madame

Rigobert would not have failed to make—no, he merely had a very clear sentiment of his unworthiness, and that his house did not deserve to be so glorified.

"Let's go see the King," he proposed, after some hesitation.

She acquiesced with a nod of the head.

He had found nothing better: the King—and yet, since he had professed for his master until then the pure fidelity of a valet, he could not have said whence there came to him now, for that illustrious personage, a strange and invincible scorn. But after all, he was the first man in the land—and then, the lady had accepted . . .

They went.

What motive did Rigobert obey when, respectfully, some distance from the palace, he took back from Truth the rich rags that travestied her?

When the door as opened he sent word—he was a chamberlain of the top flight, who had access to the monarch at any hour of the day or night—he sent word that he had very grave things to communicate to His Majesty.

Scarcely had those words been proffered, however, than, before the henceforth ineluctable necessity of presenting to the King that woman imperiously clad in her beauty, the woman who had made him a new being with a glance, Rigobert felt his courage abandoning him, and he fled—with no regard for etiquette!—as fast as his legs could carry him.

The King did not wait . . .

(To introduce you to him: an excellent scoundrel. A strong head, I swear to you, and a fellow who had formed of life, and particularly of royal life, a certain idea, and who steered himself through the clutter of government with a perfect equanimity. On his subject, legends had run around, accredited, if not justified, by the celebrated and fatal beauty that the man enjoyed, even though he had passed the extreme limits of decrepitude a long time ago. In whispers, people said that he was none other than Herod Antipas, the one to whom Jesus was sent before being delivered to the Jews and the one who had John the Baptist decapitated. I cannot affirm that, but he was, for sure, the most honorable rogue I have known. He had a long blond beard and never took off his gilded crown.)

As soon as he saw Truth he frowned, tugged his beard and ground his teeth—in sum, giving all the classic signs of the most violent wrath.

"You!" he growled. "You again! And this time, Yourself!"

The beautiful woman looked at him, placid and disdainful, as if he had only been his own chamberlain.

He cried: "Speak! You're Truth, aren't you?"

She opened her arms wide, in a cross. "It's you who said it!"

The King sniggered and sat down.

"Well, then," he said, "What do you want with me? For you've been persecuting me for centuries. The time before last you took the form of an old man and, as president of the tribunal of Archontes, I thought I'd get rid of you by condemning you to drink from the poisoned cup. But four centuries later you appeared to me again and your audacity had increased. The young man whose face you borrowed claimed to be a king! Since the days of Athens I had improved my position, and the simple judge had become a Tetrarch; it appears that we grow together through History, you and I; I am the King, and you finally dare to show yourself in your sovereign splendor! Well . . ."

At this point the King stood up and bowed deeply.

"Well, Majesty, my Cousin, be very welcome!"

He burst out laughing.

"Ha ha! You didn't expect that, eh? For once, I'll no longer have the naïveties of old. You have the keys to all the doors of the tomb, Madame, and martyrdom is your ally. Forget the road to the prison and Calvary, then; I'll render you all the honors that are due to you. Your place is in the Temple, in the most secret retreat of the sanctuary; I'll take you there—and you'll be well guarded!"

"King Lie," said Truth, with a tone of arrogant pity, "it's doubtless necessary that you consummate your own damnation. Now, I swear to you by Myself that an hour will chime when humanity will comprehend that your priests sacrifice me, in effect, every morning in their holy sacrament, and will come to snatch me from their hands and purify the Temple."

The King shrugged his shoulders.

The next day, conducted by thirteen incurable deaf-mutes commissioned to guard her, Truth was sequestered in the Holy of Holies, and the priests continued to spread their immemorial teaching of error.

But in the evening of the same day, strange news reached the ears of the King, although he rubbed his hands together in the fashion of his friend Pontius Pilate.

A man, it was said, who wore tattered clothes of silver and gold, was running around the streets and crossroads gathering crowds and exciting them to scorn the present order of things: the absolute power of the King was illegitimate and the doctrine of the priests diabolical; lies and corruption were polluting the air, and forgetfulness of the eternal Truth was leading the world to the definitive abomination.

The man was arrested without delay and taken to the palace, where the King wanted to interrogate him personally.

"Who are you?"

"I have no idea," replied Rigobert, "and haven't I changed a lot, since you aren't able to recognize me? Yesterday, I was your servant—which is to say, a wretched debauchee who ran after you to endless misfortune. Today, disabused because I've contemplated the glorious visage whose sublime splendor ought to have converted you too, I'm expiating the past by devoting myself to human salvation. And it's necessary for you to hear me! King, it's time for penitence!"

"Imbecile!" said the King.

He summoned the judges, and when they had come, he said: "Messires, I deliver to you the most detestable of criminals. He claims to be speaking the truth; laugh a little! Like me, Messires, you know that there are two truths: the one that we shall never know, for it will only ever be proffered through the mouths of children who do not talk yet; and the other, the serious, official truth that we practice every day, which we find—do we not?—good."

The judges nodded in assent.

"That solid truth, Messires, is the cornerstone of the entire social edifice. It is a rational convention that dispenses us from any dolorous research and permits us to savor with certainty the joys of life. That convention has many names: habit, politeness, modesty, politics . . .

"Thanks to that convention, people who detest one another approach one another with all the exterior marks of the most urgent affection. Thanks to that convention, to the desire to know, to dangerous questions, we can oppose the victorious response of the universitarian routine, a response confirmed by the diplomas we print, symbolically, on donkey-skin. Thanks to that convention, the overly grave problems of psychology or public morality are stifled by the imposing noise of governmental mechanisms . . .

"But what is the point of listing the benefits of the truth, such as it is understood? Is not denying it, Messires, to deny the light of day?"

The judges nodded assent.

"However, Messires, this man, in the name of the other truth, the unknowable one, has had the audacious sacrilege of denying the official truth. He was one of my most useful servants; I do not hesitate to sacrifice him to the public interest.

"You will condemn him to death, Messires," concluded the King, in a thunderous voice, "for he is the enemy of the peace of the world, and, in order that his example will impose upon everyone the love of the true and the horror of the false, on the cross on which he will be hung you will write with his blood: BECAUSE HE LIED."

# NABUCHODONOSOR

> I will ascend into heaven,
> I will exalt my throne
> above the stars of God; I will
> sit also upon the mount of
> the congregation, in
> the sides of the north.
> *Isaiah* 14:13[1]

THE PALACE darts its towers arrogantly toward the heavens, its hundred towers of Babel, toward the heavens, which laugh, from the depths of their impassive eternity, at the immeasurable pettiness of the hundred towers.

. . . It is in a city in the Bible and perhaps also in those times, a city of all races and all seasons, devoid

---

[1] The speech is credited in the A.V. to "Lucifer, son of the morning," apparently meaning the king of Babylon doomed by the (somewhat gnomic) prophecy contained in the relevant chapter. The protagonist of the story is more familiarly known as Nebuchadnezzar II, king of Babylon from c605 B.C. to c562 B.C., who is said to have behaved irrationally in his later years, and whose death was the prelude to Babylon's conquest by the Persian King Cyrus the Great.

of history, a city of legends such as one divines written in the grace and emphasis of monuments, with lyrical steeples everywhere, darted at the clouds. But none of the many gigantic architectures dares to rival the House of the King. It is situated at the center, a sublime spider, and the streets emerge like threads from the hundred doors that the hundred towers design.

Everything protects her and she governs everything, the true queen. And for forgotten centuries she has been the reliquary of strength and virtue, glory and grandeur; and for centuries, welcoming and sumptuous, she testified even more generosity, the beloved, than she excited amour; and for centuries she has been installed there like a great testimony to human greatness . . .

But what is being said? What has abruptly altered the color of the sky above the arrogant towers? It is said that the Palace has swollen with the pride of its strength and its virtue, its glory and its grandeur. An *excessively* enlightened monarch has taken his place on the old throne for five years, during which, day by day, the sky has darkened above the arrogant towers, and the people are forgetting, day by day, to laugh softly as they were once accustomed to do, in the times of kings infatuated with bellicose glory, proud of loving, good servants of beauty, joyful in reigning and living.

However, the present crown-bearer surpasses in wisdom, it is certain, the purest heads with which his lineage is illuminated. Why does his venerable name weigh upon all the people like a condemnation, and why do gazes not dare to address themselves to the doors of the Palace without sacred horror?

※

The Palace darts its hundred towers arrogantly . . .

In the surrounding area, the squares and crossroads are black with people, black with innumerable people who are clamoring, clashing swords, excited, agitating banners, who are crying, as if for help: "The King! The King!" and hammering on the doors of the Palace with their fists.

The Palace is deaf and blind, the agitation of all of that crowd has no echo in the disdainful towers. Except that, from time to time, a valet opens his servant's door to make imploring gestures of appeasement at the mutinous mob.

For a thousand days now the King has refused the adoration of his people. The King is neglecting his royal duties, abandoning his people to the knavery or indolence of irresponsible ministers.

Oh, the populace can appeal and become irritated; its demands occupy the King as much as the murmurs of the sea and the ordinary tumults of life . . .

It is said that for a thousand days he has been enclosed in the most profound of the vast chambers of his palace; it is said in whispers that for a thousand days, he has been face to face with a phantom of God. Since his youth he has been infatuated with the tenebrous promises of the

Kabbalah, and Sages summoned from far away marveled at one greater than Solomon.

Gradually, he has sequestered himself in the solitary honor of being a Seer. Now, disinterested in his ancestors' dreams of glory and blood, having lost his taste for loving, surfeited with living, weary of reigning, he has become some inhuman heap of thoughts. Legendary in his own lifetime in the mystery that shelters him from curiosity, he appears to mortals as something unnamable, august and redoubtable, the form of which, being sacred, remains vague.

And the Palace, which had waited a long time for such a guest, is like the natural habitat of the omnipotent silence: a sumptuous edifice, as if fictitious in always being closed; a massive and inexhaustible receptacle of the shadow that it projects afar, like a reflection of its depths, a monumental vestment of a formidable being.

However, that vestment of granite, bronze, marble and precious stones, an entire people drunk on abandon has sworn to tear apart. The City, the City-Without-End, is also weary, and also surfeited with the hideous consolations that it has sought in all its debaucheries: a monstrous Sodom, already in haste to mirror its ruinous grandeur in the mirages of Asphaltite, because it has no longer had the joy, for a thousand days, of listening to the song of its living blood that once flowed delightfully from the Palace, as from a vast heart.

In order to extract the King from his criminal apathy, the City has imagined declaring war on the nearest Gomorrah, and already the dangerous enemies have agitated the inflamed banners in the country . . .

Let the King show himself! It is time!

"The King! The King!"

If not under amorous hands, you will fall, O Palace, under infamous and victorious hands! Open up! The people are powerful in number and desire, and have not found a goal in the pleasures into which the royal treason has precipitated them, and, since the King sees God, the people are jealous to participate in the vision of God. The people are great; it is from the God himself, from the God who seems to have abandoned them, that they want to steal the glory of the divine vision, and of the Thrones and the Dominations, and the deaf Heavens: the Heavens that laugh from the depths of their impassive eternity, at the immeasurable pettiness of the people.

The battle howls and fumes at the gates of the City. Men without arms and children flee, their hands spread in horror, and cast trouble into the battalions that have formed. But why? Victory is certain, since the King is the divine elect. Let him only show himself, the royal deserter!

The army of Amazons, a lascivious and beautiful multitude, bellicose, pitiless and invulnerable, it is said— for wounds exasperate and do not stop those demons, a multitude like a stormy rain of lances—the well-led army rolls through the City the frightful din of machines of war. Can it be that the racket is not audible in the Hundred Towers? And the people, desperate, fall almost without defending themselves any longer, under the rhythmic thrusts of the furious women.

"The Enemy!"

"The King!"

Those two cries mingle, and are they not the same cry? Is not the same one, also, that immense cry of agony that fills the proud city, the city traversed and swept in all directions by the vast flood of carnage?

And the Heavens laugh, from the depths of their impassive eternity, at the immeasurable pettiness of the massacre.

※

The Killers have stopped and gathered at the foot of the Palace that darts its hundred towers of Babel toward the heavens. And laughter, enormous laughter, diabolical laughter, dishonors the echoes of the ancient dwelling; the laughter of victory from below, the laughter of mud thrown in the face of statues. And the doors, once obstinate in silence, groan under the formidable effort of catapults and battering rams.

The immemorial doors! The doors sculpted and painted by centuries of genius! The holy doors whose hinges rendered a harmonious sound as they rotated: what a plaint today! Oh, what sinister gasp inhabits and suddenly awakens in the profaned bronze!

And it is not the adoring violence of a faithful people that rushes and spreads through the House. The courtyards, the stairways of honor, the corridors and the halls reverberate dolorously with the clamor of the triumphant, and the humiliated flagstones weep beneath the feet that insult them.

※

Outraging hands soil celebrated portraits: old monarchs and old sages, ancient individuals consecrated by glory. Tiaras are astonished by the long and bloody tresses that they decorate. The reserve of treasures delivers like hiccups to ferocious and naïve eyes, things of which the dream alone intoxicates the imagination of the dreamer. And the most outrageous hands of all, maleficent but ignorant, take pleasure in lacerating the riches of a library unique in the world. The manuscripts of Sanchuniathon, those of Berossus, the poems of Pentaour and the hymns of Orpheus, the lessons of the Magi, the authentic texts of the Books of Thoth Trismegistus, the Revelations of Li and Ki, the Dramas of Kalidasa, the Wars of Iaveh, the Prophetic Enunciations, the Veda, the Avesta . . . in sum, all the most illustrious testimonies of our genius—and the Heavens laugh, from the depths of their impassive eternity, at the immeasurable pettiness of those lost testimonies.

"The King! The King!"

It is the enemy that is vociferating that appeal—an order!—while searching the labyrinth for the designated victim, and the vaults and the walls, with a confession of ultimate treason, repeated in a commanding tone: "The King! The King!"

That door, is it not the one that opens to the most profound of vast chambers? That door, on which mystic emblems are sculpted, dominated by the menacing visage of a gorgon? It is there that he has been, for a thousand days, face to face with a phantom of God.

The murderers hesitate, and their gazes are concerted, and their voices excited—and the door collapses.

And the women who launched themselves forward with bloody syllables stop, immobilized, mute, trembling and tottering with vertigo.

Alone, in the solitude of an atmosphere smoky with unknown essences, a being is standing, charged with a royal mantle whose pleated flaps trail on the ground to attest that the being was once taller. Stooped, head bowed—an enormous head, a monstrous head from which the crown has slipped—alone, a being is standing there, gazing toward the threshold and seeming not to see anything. He does not move. They do not know whether he is alive.

For a long time the intruders stay there, trembling and tottering, more tempted to flight than the assassination anticipated as a celebration.

But one bold woman finally approaches and leans over to consider the face that remains in shadow—and cries out, and falls inanimate, on seeing that the entire visage has been devoured by the forehead.

The eyes are weeping beneath, bestial and sad, like those of a bison; the eyes are weeping and filled with darkness, and about to be extinguished, while the nose and the mouth are two derisory streaks beneath the limitless forehead of Nabuchodonosor; and the Heavens laugh, from the depths of their impassive eternity, at the immeasurable pettiness of that forehead.

# ON THE FLOATING CANVAS...

ON the floating canvas of my sentiments at the twilight of the awakening, no longer sleeping but still dreaming, I tried to paint the image of a face once familiar to the quotidian of my life, a Visage henceforth faithful to my memories alone. And I know full well that I strove for a long time—the fictitious and true long time of dreams—without being content. So, I did not find lines subtle enough, or colors harmonious enough, for the charming name that it was necessary to inscribe in the charming semblance. If, sometimes, I was about to applaud myself for some certainty, to recognize beneath the dolorous sketch the amorously sought form, an invisible, jealous hand immediately corrected and altered my work, and I observed, at each new defeat, oh, I observed with annoyance that another face had been substituted on the floating canvas—ever more clearly—for my desire. A visage of yesterday and today, dear once to the error of an amour in which I was deceived, today watching, still malevolent, my dolors and my faults; why is it obstinate, an accomplice of life, in chasing away the one that is only any longer faithful to my memories? Why does it seem to desire again, quite frivolously, to seduce the disenchanted lover? Phantom of a dream, is it merely that a capricious recurrence of our former pleasures had, in this twilight if awakening, recalled the soul devoid of beauty once adored in the lie of a lovely face?

In a voice of tender melancholy, feigning obedience: "Here I am, what do you want with me?"

I avoided responding. I concentrated all the energies of my heart and mind in the chosen evocation: but in the end, the importunate visitor, the intruder, installed herself in her detested authenticity, and then . . .

"No!" I cried. "Don't hasten to triumph; I'm not allowing myself to be defeated. What do you get out of this hypocritical game of servitude? Your fantasy that you seemed worthy of being respected by my desire is of no importance to me, and you're quite wrong to come and console my solitude if you don't know to what you're exposing so much devotion. You're there, it's really You . . . what is it, then, 'You'? Whatever you believe that to be—and who would dare to conclude that you can be anything other than that to me, O improvident, O forgetful, O multitude!

"When it was pleasant for you to love me, the strangers that crossed your path only offered you, even on their knees, living pretexts for making your idea of me more precise; they evoked me by virtue of the very fact of not being me; for: 'Is that the way *he* walks, *he* smiles, *he* shuts up?' In your view, their entire reason for being was constituted in me, in that they reminded you of me by way of harmonies of discords, and you had destituted them of themselves. Well, you in your turn, you too—a specter of pasts that I've denied—who come with the wishes of another time, you too, be appointed *someone other than yourself,* who only exists for me insofar as you suggest someone else!

"Each of your features, which all pretend to betray my expectation, fixes those which I was expecting. Your eyes, illuminated by mediocre cares, dazzle me with the spiritual light that flowed between eyelids now closed. That mouth of a pretty slave, one who does not know the eternal syllables, retakes the rebellious curve of lips that said: 'I give myself and I stay.' That narrow forehead proclaims the glory of the unique Forehead where the purest of my thoughts was purified further. You are only manifest in favor of a comparison, you are the victory of whom you thought to vanquish, you resuscitate, fool, the one you thought to relegate to the blackness of the crypt.

"And it's you who are dead! This portrait of you, which varies incessantly, this impertinent image of an emanation of your coquetry, is the portrait of a dead woman, since you vary incessantly, living woman, since—even sparing the parallel in which you succumb—you are *someone other than yourself,* perpetually and essentially. Whereas, stripped of the reflections that belie the light clouds in the sky of life, the one who is only any longer faithful to my memories remains inviolable there, constant, like a statue on the shore of the wave of your changes."

# NARCISSUS

THE CHILD grew up under the gaze of the grandmother in the ancient dwelling in which, by a prodigy of prudence and fidelity, everything save for him was ancient. In the sumptuous halls, on the historic flagstones, between the ornate tapestries in which the family history was perpetuated from the dusks of the past from the dawns of the future; in the silent park, among the domesticated deer and the old white and black swans with the slow, gentle lines; in the austere Gothic chapel where the late Baron, his father, in the costumes of war, and his dead mother, in a festival gown, knelt before the venerable images of their blessed patrons; in the forest of dense darkness, between his ferocious greyhounds and his rapacious birds of prey, with the savage perspective of the Pyrenees far beyond, the child grew up, various, long motionless, taciturn, abruptly carried away by the hazard of vagabond courses, to the dithyrambs of inexhaustible soliloquies: as various as the instants of an April day, capricious and grave, and he was always ignorant of the gaiety of games in which the turbulences of assembled children expand in pleasant follies.

Sometimes, he considered with an innocent, serious and questioning gaze the lady of unknown age who reigned in that empire of prudence and fidelity, the immemorial soul of that narrow world closed to new vanities.

And as he grew up, she summoned, in order to lighten the heavy concern of the education of a man, priests with hair like falling snow. Doubtless without haste, those patriarchs enclosed the thoughts of their noble pupil within the limits of the wisdom of the early days, as well as communicating to him a little of their decrepitude. First they informed him of all that is imprescriptible in the precious prejudices of Tradition to the hazardous awakening of a very ardent mind. Scarcely was that coat of mail well-fitted than he was launched into the melee of human knowledge. His vivacious anxieties converged avidly on that multiple shadow of the unique prey. He pored over theologies, philosophies, histories and geometries; even his dreams were learned; a despotic curiosity was all of his passion, and his masters trembled, foreseeing that one day soon he would leave them far behind in that vertiginous hunt for the truth, on the ultimate edge where the beaten paths cease.

Now, the white-haired lady, in delivering the mind of her grandson and that tremulous precocity to exceedingly old magi, had reserved for herself the protection of his heart and scarcely opened senses. She awaited, with the experience of a woman and the divination of a mother, the frisson of the dawn of nascent desire that troubles and does not dare. Perhaps instructed, in some distant past, of the perils of living too rapidly, she was a jealous guardian of that adolescent candor. Mirrors in which the young man's beauty might have smiled were proscribed.

Life in the château was rude, all long toil and harsh exercise. Early on, with the fire of scruple and religious commandments, a disdain was ignited in the child for his corporeal graces, with the result that his gaze was never tempted to take pleasure in the masculine mildness of his forms, of a young hero. But the grandmother could not forbid herself the pleasure of combing his long blond hair, which was like the freshness of a bright summer night around the radiant midday of his visage. And while the hands lingered, besotted, in the rich curls, he dreamed.

Was that grandmotherly tenderness hiding some lure of pride? Was it to human astonishment that the marvel of such a beautiful being was dedicated? Or perhaps— and once and for all before the end of mankind!—to the accomplishment of human perfection? But, to good, wicked or indifferent Nature, did she also want to add the collaboration of the work of choice, in conferring on the elect of science and beauty the redoubtable gift of physical consciousness?

After he had exhausted on many hills the grapes of the vines of Science, the young man closed his books and left the insulting dust to powder them with forgetfulness in his study. He went into the forest, with the dusk, with the darkness; with his head bowed he walked for a long time. He dreamed.

From the world glimpsed on the edge of all the mysteries, a veiled figure had suddenly loomed up, and that apparition had thrown back into shadow all the mysteries of the world. With a tranquil terror, as if he had always known that it was necessary that the veiled figure would loom up before him at a certain moment, the young man had recognized it as his own mystery. And because that phantom had suppresses other contingencies for him, that alone made him think. Like an angel on the threshold of paradise, the phantom standing on the threshold of the House of the World said: "Further beyond are the sweet secrets; but in order to reach them it is necessary to lift or tear my veil."

And the strange words awakened a thousand voices in his opening soul, which said: "For the key to the great House is *you*, and without it you will roam its surroundings in vain, *without you*. The Questions are consonant and resolved in you. You, in your tangible reality, are the crossroads of the World. Seek the Answer in the beating of your heart, in the dreams of your life, in the eloquence of your gestures. Before pursuing risky pilgrimages to distant shores, to inhospitable shores, obtain advice of yourself."

Thus commenced to appear in the young man's will, like a torch of increasing light on the horizon of the desires of puberty, the project of learning his soul and knowing his body: his body, that interesting spectacle, that sanctuary of intimate verities.

Everyday things, not inspected before, touched him tenderly. He enjoyed, as a novelty, the elasticity of his stride, the caress of his hair. His hands loved one another, clutching one another. The habitude of chastity lent to frail details a price of rare charm. From the ease of his movement, the intoxication of health rose to his brain. His feet took possession of the earth in walking thereon, his gaze took possession of landscapes. He breathed the air sensually, a conquest of the sky. Yes, what a joy it was to see in his entire self the illumination of revelation!

And much more ardently than in the days of childhood, his questioning eyes scrutinized the savant and challenging eyes of the grandmother, seeking a living mirror therein. But she, tremulous, and fearful of understanding, closed her pallid eyelids.

She had frequent conversations with the old men, in which she sometimes raised an accusatory voice, reproaching them for having betrayed her design. Why had he wearied of study? Was it not because the masters lacked knowledge or devotion? The old men humbly raised the objection of the fatal fever of a youth perhaps too long suppressed, they suggested, and a warm blood rendered impatient by constraints.

And those saddened men and that heartbroken woman, kneeling in the chapel, implored the Very Merciful to remove the menacing probabilities.

One day, the one who cost so many dreads and prayers, one glorious summer day, the young man traversed the park singing. Seeing him cheerful, everything became cheerful. His greyhounds bounded; the swans on the lake rippled the water more rapidly, where the willows were no longer able to distinguish their tearful branches. He traversed the forest at a run, all the way to the limits where the sheer mountains were revealed.

A marsh was dormant in the profound forest. Huge elms cradled it with interlacements. It was a deserted place unknown to furtive hinds and flocks of sparrows. In the depths of the water there was a glaze of mud, the soft natural silvering of a liquid mirror, a calm and fresh mirror in which the floating phantom of the trees was reflected.

It was a deserted place, secret and religious, a place predestined for the accomplishment of some redoubtable amorous ritual. The light filtered through the foliage, over the dead water, the smiles of life.

Without turning his head, freed from the tranquil terror once emanated by the veiled figure, delivered now to the victories of desire, now that the delightful specter promised to allow itself to be seen, Narcissus, his forehead rosy with the emotion of his voluptuous enterprise, undressed himself slowly, his gaze lost in the distance of a joyful dream.

Slowly, he came to the edge of the marsh where destiny awaited him; slowly, and as he had once pored over bleak books, he leaned over his image. Could he not adore you, image of his youth? And adoring you, too abruptly and without initiation, O murderer, O shattering revelation, could he not exhale, in his last and first sigh of amour, his entire soul?

# AND I AM THE ONE OF YOUR SOULS...

AND I am the one of your souls, of your most baleful souls, of the desperate days of abandonment, which went away, having cast over everything that you were an angry gaze, over the hours that will never return, the hours that became knells, which sounded so much of life, and over the hour that vibrates, ringing false, it is said, an unreal appearance, and over the hours that might perhaps sound in the future, greatly discounted—which went away to a bleak land of which legends had informed it, where there is, in a landscape that three exceedingly old birches impregnate with solitude, an ancient well with edges worn away by generations: it is the Well of Maledictions; and whoever dies a bad and sad death, his name will have been pronounced in the resounding night of the millennial well, as is attested, for the quivering horror of the living by numerous examples that tradition reports. And I am the one of your souls, the most baleful of all, which, on a day of abandonment, leaned over the worn rim of the Well of Maledictions in order to drop your name into its resonant darkness.

## THE SILENCE SUBSIDES . . .

THE SILENCE subsides; one might think that lips were untightening. In the profound lake of the mirror, everything is troubled, and the madman—oh, the madman!—feels alone, as before, as always, with the living soul that the dead have left him. The atmosphere becomes calmer; it is no more than ordinary folly; and on the table, over there, under the light that springs forth and falls back of an intermittent flame that consumes itself, is the page commenced . . .

And he smiled a distracted smile at that recall to the task. Better the solitude of old than the terrible round of regrets, reproaches and remorse . . .

But what is that sad sound, now? One might think it an infant weeping—and in the darkness of the street, a dog is howling in the distance; one might think it the cry of a damned soul. Is it the end? Is it the promised malediction? Is it the last plaint of memory?

"O my God, immense nucleus with neither place nor date, toward which the desire of my soul always tends, like a spark recalled to its origin, in spite of the vague sound of the hours, distract from my path the shadows of the past, that I might only live toward the future, in the absolute forgetfulness of the living and the dead! May I only live in aspiration toward your light, in the absolute forgetfulness of forms and bodies! May I only live in the spiritual love of your beauty, in the absolute forgetfulness of women and men!"

## HAVE YOU LIVED . . . ?

HAVE you lived your days? Oh, the future has harmed you already, you have already formed the project of living, and living life has already escaped you! And now, just as mad, you return to that past, which, for that very reason, had no reality. Do you recall your infantile eyes?

People said that they were so big, so beautiful! Everything was reflected therein, everything was mirrored therein, and, seen in them, everything was charming. Old men said that in the depths of those eyes shone the lighted torch of revealed Secrets. Perhaps your soul had already attained the evil of hope, but it had not yet depraved your virginal eyes, your infantile eyes.

When they opened after slumber, so blue did they reflect the blue sky that sages said that those eyes had stolen from the sky its most real reality. And they also said: Babels and balloons seek in vain to puncture the clouds: madness! Oh, crime and folly! It is not with hands that it is necessary to attain the sky; it is with our eyes, with our beautiful eyes; and is it not entirely attained and realized, measured by our kisses, in the adorable eyes of infants?

Your eyes knew the sky by virtue of the sublime human animality that exalted within you, but perhaps your soul had already set forth on the journey toward the Babels and balloons, to go to seek in the distance the sky that was, however, in your eyes! And it is a very little thing, it is nothing, for you to know that you possessed the sky, for you cannot render it; never again, never again will you be the child that you were; like everyone else, you no longer have anything but balloons and Babels. Pride, it is true, which will soon burst forth on your forehead, will affirm that you alone will finally build the marvelous tower on which God will come and lean, in order to consult man.

Your eyes were fragments of the sky; they poured out peace and joy, and your prettily useless hands played with sand, seashells and flowers . . .

You had the eyes of children who will not live! So, have you lived your days? Scarcely! They come back to you as to another, they are strangers to you. You raise your head from the book, you gaze vaguely, and, seeing a blue gleam on the horizon, you say to someone who is not there: "Do you recall my infantile eyes?"

# EVERYTHING GOES AWAY

I

*Everything goes away, leaves me, bids me adieu. Everything bids me a single adieu.*

The image haunts me of a Ship with beautiful sails in a good wind, sails aloft and anchor lifted, and the pride of very distant adventures. No movement, however, the Ship is inert, inert in its girdle of waves, inert the beautiful Ship, and the Land goes away, the nurse-Land leaves it . . . a long adieu . . . the Land, the Land draws away with its sacred hills, the Land of strong men and charming women goes away from the beautiful Ship. A strange departure! And the handkerchiefs shaken in the port . . .

*Everything goes away, leaves me, bids me adieu. Everything bids me a single adieu.*

You think: illusion; the ship is traveling well, traveling so rapidly that one thinks that one sees the shore fleeing . . . No! I say that the shore is veritably fleeing, I say that the Land is going away, going away. This is a nightmare! Oh, and here's another, now: the Land is coming back, the fortunate land! the port has reformed, I recognize it with the promises of shores. I recognize the women and the men who are marching and singing near the joyful waves. And beyond, there is the infinity of an enchanted garden . . .

*Everything goes away, leaves me, bids me adieu. Everything bids me a single adieu.*

It is an immense garden with blue hills in the distance of the air, green at sea level, with enthusiastic and sonorous fountains, a populated garden, and dear houses, and flowers, and flower beds on the thresholds for the feet of children, and also for the feet of travelers who are expected. Let them disembark, then! But . . . what travelers? The Ship with the beautiful sails has disappeared. Wrecked and sunk in the port, the beautiful Ship! Oh, the distances, the proud departures! Yes, certainly, it has gone far . . .

*Everything goes away, leaves me, bids me adieu. Everything bids me a single adieu.*

## II

And another time, it will be a troop on the march toward the lost horizon. They go past, the troopers, and look

me in the face, and the musicians, by way of a fanfare, only have voices, and sing:
Everything Goes Away. Everything Goes Away.
They are a little further on and turn toward me; the road stretches out, the voices weaken, and yet I can till distinguish with a cruel clarity the Syllables, the fateful and magnificent syllables, which are:
*Everything goes away. Everything goes away.*
One by one the turned faces disappear; there is a bend in the road, the troop has vanished. Now the melancholy refrain only vibrates very softly, and it is, I believe, in my heart that I hear it:
Everything goes away. Everything goes away.

# DEDICATION OF A BOOK OF JOY

AS in a marsh a flower, delicate and regal—oh, regal above all, the reeds, and delicate the mud—which is exalted, here, between the swarms of black funereal birds and their cries, which vibrate, here, wing and ode, my Joy!

Oh, truth of all my desire! Oh, bitterness of all my truth!

The terrible intoxication of my enchantments—the supernatural and simple world of my soul—the eternalized fête of the future dawn—voices ordering me to be happy.

*I suppose.*

Leave fallen souls to be frightened by the aspect of Revealed Beauty in the nudity of her triumphal dolor . . .

She plays with monsters and persuades them to raise their heads, to look toward the sun. She divides the solid shadow of centuries heaped up in the forgetfulness of Sense, and hands of light scatter shadow and forgetfulness. She informs in giving herself, being Joy. She takes pleasure in the charms of faces and landscapes, and dreams, gazing at them, of infinity. She signals to the Angel that it is time. She tells the ode to open the Angel's wings in order that humans will understand and learn. She has prepared the final holocaust; she gives for an example the precept of sacrifice and illustrates life with her blood, laughing. Her authority comes to her of its own accord in relation to Everything, and the aureole of the flames of dolor, the aureole on her visible forehead, the aureole of dolor promises—attesting God—the triumph of joy.

I SUPPOSE.

# IN THE FOREST

INTO the autumnal forest, a beautiful lady, into the desolate forest, a beautiful young and adorned lady, with the attitude she would adopt for crossing the threshold of a drawing room when the conductor of the orchestra has already raised his baton, into the autumnal forest, a beautiful lady has entered.

It is very musty, it is very rusty, it is very dusty.[1] The feet of pale satin and the brightly-colored robe are soon speckled, and on the noble bare shoulders, and the hair splendid with flame, it is raining leaves, it is raining little dead leaves, soundlessly, soundlessly.

The lady goes on, without choosing her footfalls, and that makes a *flic-flac* around her, and the sumptuous train of her robe has gradually taken on the shade of the desolate forest, of the autumnal forest, all musty, all rusty and all dusty, where the desolate wind, the autumnal wind, sighs in the leafless branches.

---

1 The original has *mouillée* [damp], *rouillée* [rusty] and *souillée* [soiled], but I thought it more appropriate to preserve the triple rhyme than the precise meaning.

The lady goes on—and now a handsome young man advances to meet her, in an evening costume . . . at least, one suspects that it was once an evening costume, but the forest has tinted profoundly, with its dead colors, the fine shoes and the suit that was once a calm, very correct black.

The handsome young man—was he waiting for her?—has doubtless been in the autumnal forest much longer than the beautiful lady; and they have come toward one another, and they have not smiled, and they have scarcely saluted one another; but he has put his arm, gently, around the supple waist of the young and adorned lady.

Indolently, the lady has placed one hand on the handsome young man's shoulder, and the fingers of the other she abandons to the rust-gloved fingers of the young man in what was once an evening costume, and they both turn in the steps of a waltz, to the rhythm of the desolate wind in the branches.

They twirl, and over their heads and over their shoulders, the dead leaves fall incessantly, the little dead leaves fall unendingly. The hours pass and the leaves fall, they fall and the days pass, and it is now on a deep carpet of little dead leaves that the waltzers are waltzing.

And it is now up to their knees that the carpet of leaves has risen—the leaves falling, the hours passing—and it is now in dead leaves that the beautiful lady and the handsome young man are dressed; the days pass and the leaves fall in the autumnal forest, the desolate forest.

Hasten to see the living eyes shining for the last time! So many dead leaves have rained down on the charming couple that their faces are henceforth effaced. And so many more have rained down that even the double human form—it was a young woman, it was a young man—is destroyed and annihilated.

And it is now only a heap of leaves—a heap of autumn leaves in the desolate forest—that is waltzing to the rhythm of the wind in the branches, which is waltzing—but it was a beautiful and adorned young lady, but it was a handsome young man; I have seen them, who were waltzing there—who were waltzing there . . .

# WOMAN

THE CREPUSCULAR rays that filter through, and regild, the frank blonde hair, the sonorous blonde hair, that she extends like a quivering curtain before the wide-open window, wound the shadow without dissipating it—and the shadow retreats and masses at the back of the room, and toward the back of the room one senses that the Lady's gaze is plunging, fascinated by that shadow. Her lyrical pose, her hands in her hair, the juvenile oval of her face designed in light upon the shadow, her features that one does not see, which one imagines—the lips that must be arched, the eyes that must be large, with fixed pupils, the eyebrows that must be furrowed, the forehead that must be creased, the nose with vibrant nostrils and the pale cheeks—make that face, glimpsed once in life, the frequent visitor of my dreams. And doubtless malign demons presided over the brief adventure of that apparition, for it only ever solicits my memory at times—oh, frequent, it's true—of unhealthy anxiety or pure disaster. Never, in the rare happy moments, have I dreamed of the unknown lady who extended her hair to the twilight, one summer evening, like a quivering curtain, and who stood motionless, in the attitude of an irritated sibyl, whom the God had made to wait longer than is reasonable.

# THE THOUGHT OF THE DEAD

I ALWAYS delight in the legends of cemeteries. I know several of them of which I could make pleasant couplets that one could recite over dessert: The story of Marie Lafamé, who made the resedas planted on her grave split their sides laughing. The story of the necrorastic soldier who ended up being sent to the galleys and escaped for love of a dead woman, but, having found nothing but unspeakable discomfiture on returning, perished over the sad remains. The story . . . I know lots of them. There isn't a single pathway in the old Parisian necropolises that doesn't contain its little document, and I collect them.

But yesterday, my liking for the dead was sadly specialized.

Early in the morning, with other indifferent individuals, I had to go to the definitive resting place of a man of letters—"one of our own," as every Revue put it. The journey was long. All the way, repeating the same thing to personalities, flattering egotisms, I ended up absenting myself from actuality and was cheering myself up quietly when I was subjected—with what violence!—to the funereal tolling of the bell. In haste, I made myself an *ad hoc* face.

The dead man led us to the very back, against the protective wall (the dear friend was always a great walker).

In passing, I noted names; one never has enough of them for stories and the best have disappeared from Bottin. And, always slightly absorbed in professional habits, I allowed myself to be summoned by the savor of syllables. *That name there*, I meditated, *wouldn't do for me. Someone else can make use of it. This one, I'll keep: it's in my nuance. As for that other one, I'll point it out to . . .* At that point, I started: the name of the dear accompanied, yes, the one that is henceforth exempt from the cares of our subjugated life, his name came to the lips of my thought, if I might put it thus. I did not forbid myself to accord a smile to the still-warm accident, assuredly so sad, by which we had been deprived—irremediably—of the irremediably unpublished works, assuredly very beautiful that the dear departed was carrying into the grave: his unrealized projects.

*Un-real-ized pro-jects.*

These syllables pursued me. I was obsessed with them during the speeches, all the "Adieu, dear friends," the "Rest in peaces" the "Au revoirs" the "No, you are not deads" and the "Your witnesses are heres" that streamed with the holy water over the freshly moved earth.

While the others went away, content with the accomplished chore, to their articles, their feuilletons, their poems, their gossip columns, their novels, their academic visits, their dramas, and their unrealized projects, I wandered alone among the tombs, with the vague dream that still enveloped me.

*He's finally arrived, then, the poor dear*, I thought.

I know more than one man of letters, like him already and you and me soon enough, buried in that cemetery. I avoided their tiny temples. Of all of them I knew the published works, and of more than one, certain designs that had not seen the light of day. Were they, those ideas whose still-future caress had rejoiced those living brains, buried with the fragile carcasses? What becomes of unrealized projects: the thought of the dead; the thought of dead ideas? Do ideas die? Do dreams, the pride of creating within ourselves, in the secret intimacy of evolutions and desires, finish there? The bitter pleasure of choosing, among our fictions, the most beloved, the most beautiful and carrying them within us for a lifetime (awaiting . . . awaiting what, alas? What?) only to narrate them to the larvae of the cemetery! And yet, is not that long wait, that implied pact with eternity, that patience of the genius who cannot foresee its end, having forgotten its commencement, the sole honor that makes life worthwhile? The misery of the care of days, not allowing them to go by in vain, empty, without appeal to races to come, without testimony before God! Well, my death will testify for me! (If I can choose!)

The mild thought of the dead, temperate absinthe, temperate in its bitterness, of which Christians and Muslims advise imbibing a little every day, as a preparatory potion for the term of a destiny inevitably humiliated in the mortuary humus—the mild thought of the dead . . .

If I were a romantic, I would lift the stones of those sepulchers at the stroke of the agonizing dusk. One would see a skeleton loom up from each tomb, still agitating the shreds of once-sumptuous garments. The landscape would be decorated by the specters of autumnal trees, and I would put the moon into it. The distant cry of a dreaming owl would give the signal, and my dead, inveterate poets, would allow to flow from their wide laughing mouths a flood that nothing would any longer retain, of miraculous words that they had come, when alive, to say to the living, and which they had not been able, specters still torn by regrets, to say to the miserly echo of the distant cry of the dreaming owl. A clock would throw over all of that the fantastic silence of midnight.

If I were a naturalist, I would descend, with a little phenol and precautions, into these crypts where the defunct are decaying, and I would calculate, in accordance with reliable formulae, how much phosphorus remained to glow in the heap of sterilized skulls. The fetor of the place would drive me away, and I would climb back up among the living with an inglorious conception of humanity.

I am neither a romantic nor a naturalist, and I think again, with a sadness that no longer wants to tolerate smiles, that thought, that mild, sickly and sweet thought of the dead, and I, would struggle between the overly precise regret of time gone by and uncertain hopes, and I doubt—oh, so much doubt!—and I am tempted, in truth, to go and throw ironic and sincere flowers of immortality on the scarcely filled-in grave of my companion, who used to sit up late with me at a tavern table; and then I shall go back, I shall go back to that supplier of the cemetery, the City; I shall go back fully possessed by the impatient memory of the projects that he, already asleep, and I, still awake, will agitate together, which his death has betrayed, and which I have not yet realized.

# THE SERGEANT AND INFINITY

WE were three friends, cheerfully going along the streets up High Montmartre at midday in spring. The City is beautiful, seen from the hill, oh, certainly more beautiful than when seen at the close range. One admires from a distance what one trudges over with ennui. The Distant, the synonym of the Beautiful . . . That day, the Distant, softened by slow mists, had such profound grace, tenderness and languor that it was unfamiliar to us again. Like an immense feminine presence, simultaneously voluptuous and majestic, animal and sublime, the expanse rejoiced religiously. And Paris blossomed in the sun: a flower whose delightful suburban countryside was the corolla.

Gazing, motionless, we fell silent in order to see better.

"Stop, thief!"

That cry, immediately multiplied, scarcely troubled our contemplation. It was enough that only one of the three of us turned round—only for a second—and we returned to the divine comedy of space, far more impassioning than the farce, even if it turned tragic, of the street.

For the event itself, a banal incident, some "assault on property," and then the pursuit of the thief, perhaps the more robbed to the two, by the wronged party, soon assisted by policemen and those benevolent bailiffs' helpers, a frightful race with which every city is overflowing, we all knew to the point of the most tedious satiety, while none of us would have been able to say—even though a logic presides over those celestial games—to what delicate series of faded tints the sunlight was about to treat the City in order to make the glory of that splendid minute pass without any violent deviations from gold to mauve, to wine-lees, to violet and to the crimson of dusk.

The hare must, however, have passed behind us, but so rapidly, it is necessary to believe, that the pack had lost the trail. We sensed the latter agitating behind us in several directions, coming and going, and then cries—"This Way!"—"No, that way!"—and then the intervention of a few between the landscape and us, in order to try to perceive what could possibly interest us more than a street in turmoil.

Suddenly, a fat sergeant, panting and crimson, out of breath, ran straight up to our group barking "Where? Where?" His imperious gesture demanded of us, doubtless as the only witnesses to the offence, an indication of the route that the thief had taken.

At that moment, a bistre cloud with two fiery points and the vague general configuration of a dragon rose up in the depths of the sky. The first of us to perceive it, pointed at it and exclaimed "Oh! Out there!"

The sergeant pounced on the gesture.

"Understood!" he said. Only then did we perceive that the man had spoken to us, *and that we had replied*, and we followed him, not without joy, curious to know how the bistre dragon would defend itself against a sergeant who, on our instruction, was about to chase it, in order to arrest it, into infinite space.

# THE INDICATOR

ONE MORNING of idling and waiting in one of those Parisian covered passages, which are the dangerous connecting links between the streets and the boulevards, having stopped at the window of a shop of "objects d'arts" I considered its repulsive products.

There were, on "boxes" devoid of utility, silhouettes of obscenity.

I considered . . .

They were, under the pretext of elegance, rubbish: prints borrowed from old masters—whose boldest caprices remain chaste because of beauty—betrayed by the libidinous care of execution, or, quite simply and without any allegation of esthetics, solely with a view to inciting old men and very young men to belated or premature labors, a sad exhibition of globes of the forestage or backstage, in bleak offertory poses.

And I considered, semi-conscious of the vile employment of minutes . . .

Suddenly, beyond the window, in the display, precisely on the object where my gaze was forgetting itself, a finger came to settle, white, tapering and feminine; and where it settled, it stayed.

What words can describe the strange fear that was immediately induced in my soul, so suddenly questioned by the unexpected Indicator, and suddenly surprised *in flagrante delicto* in stupidity and scatology?

The simple explanation—the designation by a shop-assistant to some invisible client inside the shop of the turpid futility that the idiot was about to purchase—did not cross my mind, and I stood there, ashamed, frightened and captive sensing the Finger—diabolical or divine—weighing upon my conscience.

And it was with a real sentiment of escape, of deliverance, that I fled, when, finally—and only then—the Finger was raised from the sad buttock upon which my gaze was, alas, riveted, and upon my gaze, my remorse . . .

# THE SQUARE

HOW LONG had I been considering that man, sitting a few paces away, facing me, on a bench like mine? And why did I suddenly notice that I was considering him? We sometimes pass from the state of unconsciousness to the state of consciousness without a sensible transition, and it is not only as if we were suddenly woken up with a start from some absorbing dream, immediately evaporated as soon as the eyes are open, but as if we were our own awakener, not in the secret of the dreams that were retaining us beyond the visible . . .

So, I was considering that poor worker, sad and poor, old and poor, with features that might once have been handsome, noble and respiring hope, but now we're all going downwards, toward the fall, toward the end, with the slack chin and the arched back, with the tearful wisps of gray hair escaping from the cap, with the gaze, with the thought . . .

Never, it seems to me, had I seen a face express so clearly the desert sentiment of a soul abandoning itself, the irremediable evil of renunciation.

The trees—a square is a place, the future of forests, where the city hospitalizes trees—poured over that man the green light of a mild autumn afternoon. Young women, lively in their hour's break, were going past that man with smiles, and some with songs, on their lips. Children were playing around the man, as quarrelsome as sparrows.

"It isn't for me that the sun is shining; it has shone for me. Now, it's for these girls and their lads. I too, have tucked up fresh skirts, a long time ago . . . and I too have known joy, a long time ago, in hearing children laugh who were mine. I too . . . a long time ago . . . but now . . ."

"Oh, my poor comrade, my friend, my relative! Do not even tears remain? It's good to weep."

"I too have wept, a long time ago, but now . . ."

"It's necessary not to hold it against me if I tell you this, my relative, my brother, but it really would have been better for me if I had never encountered you. And it would doubtless be better for both of us, for everyone, for you above all, who does not even have the hope of hope, if you disappeared, in order to cease to suffer and in order that no one is any longer exposed to seeing you. Your eyes are bad advice, and the air you have breathed out is not salubrious. I think I would be doing good, you'll agree, by killing you. But it's necessary not to cry for help."

At this point the wretch burst out laughing. It was not at my words—which you might deem natural—that he was laughing, for our dialogue had not passed the edge of my lips, and I alone had heard it. I truly do not know what he could have been laughing at. His laughter was frightful, hiccupping and gurgling, and he was looking at me while laughing. And it was an abominable thing, that convulsion of laughter on those features, desperate even so. It was an abominable and inconvenient thing, which certainly rendered him absolutely unworthy of dying.

"Monsieur," I said to him, in a changed tone, "I was mistaken just now, and you are not of my family. I shall therefore leave you here, on this bench, like an inconsequential larva, and I have, as you see, already got up to leave . . . However, and in spite of the profound disgust that your attitude inspires in me, if you tell me the reason for your hilarity, I will consent to reflect upon it. Not that I will go back on my decision. A man capable of laughing as you do does not merit death and I condemn you to live—for no one, be certain, will kill you if I don't. But it costs me to believe that so much dolor—you had, only a moment ago, the face of a very unhappy man—has not put a little majesty into you. It costs me to believe that the thought that is cheering you up beyond measure might be entirely ridiculous and devoid of any nobility."

As I made that speech to my wretch silently, he had no suspicion of it, and he continued laughing with the utmost impertinence. Now his entire carcass was trembling, and, although he was still gurgling, his features became dolorous again because of the contraction of the spasms. The thought occurred to me abruptly that he was about to *die of laughter*, and that immediately reconciled me with him. I even held it against myself that I had not divined his secret design, and I sat down again, very interested.

Now he was writhing, literally gasping. The conclusion was approaching, and it appeared to me to have a sublime logic.

"Bravo, my brother!" I cried (and I could have cried out, in fact; he would not have heard me) to the desperate laugher.

Yes, that most unfortunate of men was dying of laughter! That was very good. It was the sole slightly solid criticism that a very unfortunate man could make, of the society of which he was, I swear, the innocent victim, and of his own destiny. For it is ridiculous that one can be so very unfortunate . . .

And, prudently, dreading that my hero might not have the strength, or the logic, or the courage, or even the means, to finish it—there was already a small crowd of people round him, combining their energies to make a diversion to that excessive gaiety and "save the life" of the dying man—I went away, quite satisfied with the conclusion, which was at least rational, that I had given the anecdote in my conscience.

# SONNET

HE came there from the land of follies, a man's youth, and had found nothing therein that merited fixing his choice—which is to say that he possessed good experience, in the verified candor of which, durable happiness allows itself to be seduced.

She went there from the isle of stupidities, a woman's youth, and not one of the charming, complicated and vain trinkets with which the innumerable shelves are ornamented there had caused her gaze to pause—which is to say that she merited gravely being happy.

They were therefore dedicated to one another, each elected to the other beforehand, and they knew it, and they were seeking one another.

But in the street of life, as they were going in opposite directions, on different sidewalks, a carriage passed between them.

# THE SOCIETY FOR
# THE ENCOURAGEMENT OF GENIUS

"  Y ESTERDAY, again, old Europe envied the
... New World its admirable Suicide House—that
original, bold and sane institution in which the weary of
life find supreme consolations, and a wide choice of exits
pierced in all parts, adroit or forceful, from the cul-de-sac
of destiny. But the anxieties of the afterlife, while greatly
honoring Yankee genius, leave us with regret: what a pity
that such distinguished minds have only thought of piercing the isthmus of death, when the vital interests of active
society solicit so keenly and so insistently all ingenuities!
Let us occupy ourselves, I agree, with the discouraged
poor, and let us facilitate their means of escape from their
despair by realizing it, but let us not forget the valiant,
the strong, those who hold the future in their valorous
hands—those hands that are sometimes enchained by
dolorous circumstances. Let them fall, then, those chains,
let them be broken, reduced to dust and dissipated in the
four winds of invincible Progress! *For progress, for genius*:
such is our motto, and such is the legend inscribed on the
fronton of this edifice, Messieurs, where you have done

me the honor of inaugurating our great and generous (anonymous) Society for the Encouragement of Genius (capital: a hundred million . . . )"

Unanimous applause interrupted the eloquent orator here, and, after having had time to mop his brow, he went on:

"To democratic France, to the brain of France, to Paris, belongs the honor of this gigantic and magnanimous conception: science no longer being content, as before, patiently to add its observations and inventions together one by one, but safeguarding itself by defending from the evil hazards of life the factors of its own glory: poets and scholars.

"I could, Messieurs, convince you—at least, I hope so—of the excellence of our work by exposing to you in detail the principal theories on which it is founded. The august presence of Monsieur le Président de la République and the very honorable representatives of the principal constitutive bodies of the State alerts me that I ought, above all, to be careful not to abuse the rare, the previous minutes . . . I shall only say the essential . . ."

Having intruded by hazard into the singular and solemn gathering, without preliminary advertisement, with the perfect innocence of some passer-by, I thought I was dreaming. Inasmuch as it was possible for me to judge, from snatches of conversations caught here and there around me, as well as the pompous bluster of the speaker, it was a matter of a philanthropic society founded with the goal of facilitating for "genius" its debuts in social life.

Everyone knows that the mania in question is not new. It has already caused many generous deliria. The Friendly Society of Intellectual Credit (a stillborn project) was the penultimate maximal point in the thermometer of human folly, and nearly, I believe, attained complete success.

And the hour had thus sounded (capital: a hundred million) for solid realizations! Genius, strictly monitored by a subtle and experienced police, would no longer have the liberty of the sudden deviations that—in universal opinion—sterilize it. Genius, finally recognized as a serious commodity or real capital, would enter into the common funds of public wealth: the regular exploitation of genius would be organized.

Hurrah for victorious democracy! Never, in the perpetual duel to the death in which the rare phalanx of enlightened minds and the innumerable cohort of dark beings are engaged, had the former dealt the latter a more perfidious and graver blow. A marvelous and inspired tactic, one must believe, of genius itself! Immense mediocrity involved in the protection of genius! Soldiers who will say to their captain: "Your life is too precious to us for us to permit you to risk it; henceforth, instead of leading us, you will march behind us; we shall make the way, and you will follow us."

O sublime Tartuffe of that black moment, Universal Suffrage! Speech is for imbeciles . . .

Let us, therefore, listen to the orator . . .

※

"Let no one any longer accuse humanity of negligence; it is becoming serious, economical, organized. It wants to utilize all its forces. For a long time, already, it has exploited crime and caused that capital to render a few dividends in the form, for instance, of mailbags. It now intends, no longer to lose an obol of that other capital, genius.

"A lamentable history, Messieurs, is that of genius. Sometimes because of the errors of those in whom that marvelous light is resplendent, and sometimes those of humanity itself, that inestimable treasure was, ninety per cent of the time, shamefully dilapidated.

"That history is a martyrology in which the martyr was too often his own victim. How many exquisite intelligences—principally among poets, a rather frivolous race—consumed themselves in idleness or debauchery, which they decorated with the lyrical labels of dream and amour! But also, how many serious minds—I am speaking here, above all, about scientists—saw themselves refused by their fellow citizens the social collaboration without which individual effort breaks against redoubtable obstacles and risks never being anything but a hope devoid of consistency!

"Alas, Messieurs, what do great thoughts lack in order to pass from project to realization? Very little: a monetary capital that is asleep in numerous and powerful strongboxes, a capital whose glory would be to serve thought.

"Now, between those two forces that are unacquainted—Capital and Thought—what is lacking? Again, very little: a connecting beam to link them.

"Well, that connection, Messieurs, which is, if you will permit the audacity of language, a beam of light, we are inscribing in the sky of contemporary history by founding this Society, to which your benevolent presence—not forgetting the subscriptions of the most honorable capitalists of the land—gives all the desirable characteristics of authenticity . . ."

A triple salvo of applause, heightened by bravos and cheers, was saluting these beneficent words when the most unexpected of incidents occurred.

A solemn old man—long white hair, long white beard and the austere costume of a political Quaker—stood up and, with a gesture soliciting the attention of the orator and the public, pronounced, in the silence that astonishment accorded him, these words, which appeared unusual, doubtless because of their naïvety:

"I inscribe myself against the criminal doctrine of the orator and his adherents. Genius—and I am astonished to have to remind men of the enlightened time we have reached of this elementary point—is the most monstrous of social inequalities. To protect it is to ruin the entire work of the Revolution, it is to tear up the motto that contains, in embryo, all desirable reforms: Liberty, Equality, Fraternity! What folly it is to associate the words *genius* and *progress*! One denies the other. Genius constitutes the dangerous essence of ancient errors, and, for the future, the reserve of all tyrannies . . ."

A certain malaise greeted that strange interruption. There was a silence, and then private conversations were engaged here and there. I remarked smiles of pity on more than one face, and the orator could not repress a shrug of the shoulders. To tell the truth, the grim egalitarian had just committed the worst of gaffes. He probably did not know how to read. What? Had he not understood the ironic antiphrasis of the syllables *encouragement of genius*? Did he not see—perhaps blinded, in fact, by too much light—that, in taking that protective attitude, the society was initiating the most redoubtable machine of defense, obstruction and leveling of which the diabolical brain had ever conceived the idea?

The interrupter's neighbors succeeded in containing him, and the orator continued, in general sympathy.

※

". . . It is a matter, therefore, of discerning eminent minds, of sparing them the perilous years of apprenticeship, and obtaining from them the greatest possible quantity of the best possible product.

"You will doubtless ask how our Society will distinguish genius before it is manifest? The question is legitimate. My response will, I believe, dissipate all your doubts.

"You know that we possess today the ultimate secrets of the art of knowing human beings. We have scientists who, by the inspection of a cranium, a physiognomy, the palm of a hand or a few lines of handwriting, can determine accurately the intellectual and moral value of an individual.

"Suppose, therefore, a grave company of Seven Old Men, chosen among the most notable of those scholars. At the age of eight, every French child of either sex will have the duty of submitting to the examination of those august Macrobians: a kind of Intellectual Review Board . . .

"Those arbiters, in accordance with the faculties that they observe in those children, will assign them, by an infallible and inviolable verdict to careers in harmony with the said faculties.

"The children recognized as possessed of genius will be set side, reserved to a very particular solicitude. Precious hopes of the fatherland and the world, they will certainly not be allowed to lack anything. For them, the best masters and the choice morsels; their innocence will be carefully protected, and those predestined individuals will be forearmed against the terrible evil of physical precocity. Each of them will be strictly directed in his path, sparing him the dangers of personal initiation, always so hazardous. Subversive seeds will not be permitted to develop, and healthy tradition will be rigorously respected. The young man selected by nature to be the honor and wealth of his fellows will thus be impelled very high and very far, warmed to white heat, so to speak. Not a minute lost! Think, Messieurs, how rapid the progress of humanity would be if its most powerful representatives could, from the first moment, not lose a minute for their glory and their utility!

"Such is our program.

"It goes without saying that by way of just remuneration for its expenses our society will receive 50% of the net profits of the men of genius whose productivity it will have hastened and multiplied . . ."

# OUT THERE

"IT'S time to get up, you whose motto should be—although someone else has taken it—oh, should very justly be: *too late!* It's time to ask me:

"What time is it?

"Come on, it's not raining yet, it isn't raining. Anyway, the oriole has sung. May one know where you're going, pilgrim?"

"Out There!"

"That's a long way away! Have you greased your boots? And no provisions! Come on, you'll be back in a little while, feet under the table and slumped in the chair. I know the place you call *Out There*. It's a place frequented by poetasters. It's a place of embankments and guinguettes, with golf courses. For the City, at the distance of that *Way-Out-There*, gives itself oceanic airs; the houses become waves, the trucks borrow the voice of the storm. I know, I know! Are you even going all the way to the end of your Out There? Yes? Here you are, already in the little wood that you pompously call a forest! And for the first steps, you adopt a proud attitude and a good stride. That's meritorious: no one can see you.

But no imprudence; the oriole has still sung. Listen to the wind in the treetops, which will soon make the noise of a thousand sluice-gates and groan like a population of baker's boys. Go on, I'm not anxious. You'll be back before it starts to rain."

# VISION

THE SCUM on the surface of a pond sometimes reminds me of troubled dreams. Isn't *everything* reduced, in the end, to the scum on a pond?

I was sitting in the corner of a railway carriage waiting to depart. The unfamiliar agitation of the people around me, the noise of things in the resounding station, the cruelty of the light, everything seen and heard, wounded me, and my soul curled up in a ball, like a hedgehog.

That state of soul, that of the majority of travelers, I have often thought I observed; along with their tickets, at the little window, the travelers have bought ill humor. One dare not criticize them for it, or criticize oneself. It takes a great deal of philosophy to pass without rancor from the human condition to that of a parcel. The parcel remains sensible, that's the problem; it has lost all its rights, and its duties have multiplied. Since that ambulant parcel has a label, it has to obey everyone—everyone, at least, who wears a peaked cap. There's nothing to be proud of . . .

I was waiting to depart and I was already invoking sleep, that bleak deity whose rites take an ever more considerable place in our life as the industries of locomotion progress, which scarcely do anything, in fact, except multiply opportunities for sleep.

A train was extended, parallel to mine, two tracks away from mine, waiting to depart like mine. Unconsciously, I inspected its compartments with my gaze, curious to see other ennuis, like mine, huddled in the corners. The nearest carriages were empty. I leaned out of the window; the more distant carriages were also empty, all empty . . . Ah!

In the distance, against a window, the silhouette of a face that one might have thought stuck to it: a white feminine face, surmounted by an excessively voluminous plumed hat; nose flattened against the glass, the profound black holes of eyes, seemingly of a death's-head; but the delicate firm oval was that of a young woman—and in the holes of the eyes I saw two somber flames that converged on me.

That it was simply illusion of a shadow violently cut out by the harsh chisel of electricity, I wanted to believe, to begin with, and all plausibility dictated that interpretation. What is the probability, I ask you, that a female passenger was alone in that empty train? And what about that immobility?

"A simple play of shadows," I proffered, aloud, as if to seek in the sound of my own voice the sensible confirmation of a reassuring opinion: a simple play of white light and shadow on the window.

And in order to manifest my independence I turned to the other window of my compartment without admitting to myself that I was seeking a means of escaping the haunting, albeit quite impossible, presence.

Through the other window, on the platform, there was the anxious and gesticulating crowd of travelers, all in quest of the best place: a spectacle devoid of the unexpected—and no one menaced my solitude. I tried, however, to interest myself in that movement, but could scarcely manage it. Should I look to see whether *she* was still there? Why not?

I had a slight internal shudder on observing that *she* was still there, *even though the lighting had varied slightly*. But in that case . . . it was something other than a play of shadows.

Had the lighting really varied? It seemed to me . . .

Now, with a dolorous curiosity, I considered—*that*, which was perhaps a woman and perhaps nothing. She had not budged at all, and the two somber flames were still gleaming toward me, having waited for me while I did not show myself, and having drilled into my eyes again as soon as I had put my head out of the window . . .

And sometimes: yes, I said to myself, it's a woman, a living woman . . . and sometimes: impossible, nothing, illusion . . .

Now, around that feminine pretext, memories began to dance. That woman who could not be, I recognized. The features I could not see, I saw clearly. A name, a precious name, which was the dearest of my dolors, came to my lips.

What if I were to salute her?

Tremulously, I took off my hat and I inclined my head.

I thought I saw that the immobile woman had stirred slightly, very slightly—and then, immediately, she had resumed with an exact and rigorous precision, her original attitude.

That was becoming intolerable! I wanted to touch, to convince myself; I opened the door; I got down on to the track, and I had already taken three steps in the direction of—the Unknown, when I felt myself gripped by a strong hand, while a loud, furious voice said: "Where are you going? Forbidden to cross the track!"

I tried to protest, but I was not given the time; "Get back! Or . . ."

Vaguely, I heard the redoubtable sacramental vocables: "Official report! Fine . . . !" I had forgotten that I was a parcel; I was reminded of it with no more politeness than a parcel merits, and I was put back in my place . . .

And *she* had seen, and perhaps heard! Scarcely had I sat down than I hastened to look at her.

At that moment, the train pulled away, carrying away with the carriage the play of shadow or the face.

I was not able to know, and I never will know.

The play of white light and shadow on windows . . . scum on the surface of ponds, on the profound mirror of the dead water of ponds . . . It has often seemed to me that destiny was mocking me in those mirages, and I have often thought that I observed singular relationships between them and the accidents of my life, which lend to purely physical phenomena the prophetic value of a warning.

But oh, the little white patch of a face at the window, a face departed, of which one still seeks the gaze after the adieu! Wherever some obligation takes one, one goes—chin on the shoulder, striving to see, for as long as it is possible to see! However, one goes, and the adored features, so clear at first, are simplified as one draws away, and are gradually blurred, and gradually fade away. The pink and the white of the mouth are already no more, although the eyes are still shining; but finally, they are extinguished, and nothing remains, nothing at all, nothing but the evanescent face, so precious, so moving in its vague whiteness—a little whiteness—a little white patch on the window . . .

That is my entire life, that little patch, that is everything I love! Oh, it's my entire life! When it has disappeared in its turn, I shall be alone, deserted, empty—that nothing is everything to me, that nothing, an existence and a source of existences, a conscious vibration of the infinite! But all the same, however, it is not *nothing*—any more than those fecund pallors are between the green and blue ripples of the water of pools—those pallors that are also of Amour, of the past, of the future—of life—and which are not *nothing*.

# SUBJECTS; OR, THE ONLY ONE

IT was unnecessary, then, pitiful comrade, to go to ... sit down in the benches of the Circus, where the divine horsewoman Caracola was due to appear—truly an apparition!—in the sumptuousness of lights that all, a vain pretention of lamps, emanated from her person, since you knew that you were the literal prey of desire, and without the recourse of the divine Transposition by which the poet consoles himself for the residue if he does not enjoy the whole.

It is true that your error and your misfortune mark you with dignity. You were not able to disengage the essence of the Beautiful in order to possess it; at least you saw it, enviable in that for the heap of insensible human appearances who confront without peril the disaster in which you sank!

So much did your triumph have the character of a divine fatality that that unknown-the-day-before did not acquire the glory of an evening by the prestige of beauty, genius and bravery, but rather the glory that all uncrowned heads now leave around One, which she revealed to us immediately and simply, by the necessary action of her métier, exciting in you and me the same inevitable need to participate in her light: but you were burned by it . . .

I have never understood so clearly that it is really toward the crowd that glory radiates, and not from the crowd to the glorious.

In this case, feminine and animal Glory in a double and single splendor: the fantastic and indisputable affirmation of a harmonious monster, which stupid analysis resolves into two unities; certainly not a woman and a horse—neither my senses nor my reason can consent to that—or, if I suppose that the sublime Caracola can walk with other feet than a quadruped, can even have legs other than that in order to cling to the rump or the neck of a quadruped, she is no longer Her, but one among the number that I know, who pass there from the head or the heart.

Now you, naïve fool, you wanted her in your bed and believed that you could put her there; but you only lay there with Woe.

Really: a woman on horseback between two sheets! Madman.

Naïve, you did not know that your amour had within you—was it not enough?—all of her reality, and, for having pretended to close your arms on the object of your wondrous vision, you were punished, cruelly, having found nothing in the centauress but a woman, if not evil, vulgar, insensible and vile, who had even left her beauty in the saddle. So why a centauress, not being a centaur, an exile of the ideal and certain slopes and valleys, plains and clearings that her gestures in the circus suggest to us, where the males of her tribe summon her with a sonorous hoof in order to challenge the wind with her or furnish other careers? Not without reason is the track illuminated by supernatural clarities, evocative of the site of the Elysian sun in which the splendid creature could have lived at liberty. And there, a poet, far from the alcove, where I feel sorry for you, I followed you, caught up with you, and, her peer if I wished, possessed her, while you were agonizing over only embracing the deceptive demi-specter of her!

Your misfortune, my friend, speaking accurately, is an old story, told a hundred times, but which remains to be told: a belated masterpiece.

Your misfortune: the exemplary distance measured between a man's desire and his capacity.

Your misfortune: the misfortune of all men—with only one exception.

Suppose, instead of a circus rider, you loved a socialite; it's the same case, except for a few negligible circumstances of time and place. For, no more than that miracle of elegance, will the triumph of silk, diamonds and the Smile belong to you, will there be anything tangible in what it seemed, and even what you thought, you might attain in her arms, and by mingling your steps with hers in some waltz, but only the fictitious apparition of a circus, or some Celimène, Agnes or Juliet of the stage.

Thus, the majority of the reasons for which we love, Amour sets aside by virtue of everything that it is, permits or necessitates, and belies them. The prestigious flight of a riding-crop—scarcely held, one might think, by the hand, slender at a distance, but which, on the contrary, grasps it vigorously and on which an entire body is suspended—has tamed you, and in the circle traced by the animal tamer's gesture, your soul is a prisoner; ought you, however, to augur therein the tendernesses, the blandishments, and the freshnesses that are the full price, in amour, of energies, ardors and divine furies?

I hear you: "It wasn't what she does for everyone and in accordance with professional demands that I loved, but her, and everything that revealed her to me!"

And to herself too. In the same way that a smile revealed her to everyone, clad in magnificent finery, another loves a socialite—and might regret having crossed with her the threshold of the drawing room where she left "herself," along with her reason for being.

Your misfortune, the misfortune of all men—with only one exception.

Whether it was for her fashion of making marmalade or saying: "It might rain tomorrow," if you loved her for what she showed of Dorothée, Lucile, Ophelia, Clarissa, Chimène or Berenice, you'll be disappointed.

The only one fortunate in Amour is the man who, without visible fracture, is able to break through appearances, plunge with the flight of an eagle into the most intimate depths of souls in order to bring back, like a quivering prey, the veritable being that is hidden in those depths, fearful of palpitating in broad daylight in a tender and solid embrace that nothing will ever loosen. So, there is no true love without a little anxiety . . .

And similarly fortunate, alone and universal, is the man who is able to enjoy the intangible—and a woman, through the conventional and divine Being that she wants to be in the circus, the theater or a drawing room.

For this is my secret and the gift that excepts me: that I can transpose my life, in its totality, to wherever my choice, circumstance or the moment destines it, and enjoy or suffer everything in my humanity, concentrated at the point at which *that* peripety of life is encountered

And it is that prerogative that makes the poet—even if he is not the author and he is only the actor—the sole spectator of the drama that is nevertheless dedicated to a population. Shakespeare tells that the considerable and the infantile witness stories slow to ripen, on which it is doubtless necessary for curiosity to feed, not without ulterior profit for the highest faculties; but the real words of genius, the profound ones, and their analogical resonances in the three worlds, are addressed to me, who knows how to hear them.

To me, who also knows how to see Nature unveiled; and in indigence, on the Stage, all humanly informed beauty (which designs an epoch, ours, of organized barbarity) in the silence of Shakespeare, in the vacuum produced by the enormously vain luxury of the very décors in which all talent takes refuge, but in exile. It is sufficient that the instinctive gesture of the return to nature is made, unconsciously, by the artist, even if he is maladroit, of an art never entirely separated from her—Dance!—for the sumptuous lie to vanish immediately, and for my clairvoyance to be stimulated, and I give myself and abandon myself to the sincere joys—for me, at least—of a new relation of the elementary splendor.

The essential sensuality of Dance, which causes it to search for something other than the most noble, remains its safeguard, without which nothing of what the chorus and the leading dancers do can be understood, maintaining alive an art from which the others are born and reborn.

The important thing is not to confuse—any more the circus rider, the animal tamer and the actress—the Dancer with the woman, or women, of whom she is the expressive apotheosis, being all of them in herself alone, but intangibly.

On that condition, I can enjoy without danger her terrible coquetry and her provocations; I can risk myself, invisibly, beside her and in her steps, which enlarge the stage or diminish it, according to precise laws that she promulgates with an infallible ignorance. To the drama, of which I accept the invariable apparent subject—the sexual encounter—I bring the element of myself, in order to specialize it. And with the moving interest of the rhythm, without risking loving lower down than my brain, in which all of my humanity is instantaneously concentrated, I shiver, understanding that the Woman is bound to elude my muted offered desires, in spite of the ardor of a hero and the skill of a royal archer, to elude me and my arrow with a few sly steps and leaps, because she, according to the mysterious acceptance of the divine pun verified by the necessary cosmic interpretation of any dance, has no legitimate goal except tracing on the stage, with the footlights, Rhythm and Beauty, the map of the stars, the way to the STARS!

# THE FLIES

"ARE the flies in Holland Dutch?" I thought before replying to that question from a child, and then I said: "Yes." For I had just remembered that in Paris, the flies are Parisian.

And in that décor, so different from anything that can be imagined in accordance with what a citizen of the boulevard has seen—we were in Rotterdam—the very virtue of contrast suddenly evoked in my mind that memory of Paris.

A delighted idler, as I pride myself in being, I placed my character in the abundant circle of which the divine street-hawker, always and forever the same, constitutes the center.

A mystery, on which to meditate recklessly, not without profit, is that of the anonymous, vulgar, dirty being in question, who, more often than not, inhabits the other side of the law, and possesses the virtue of "interrupting the circulation." What? He's a liar and a thief—even his mind is not his, his frightful mind, imitated in the fairground and inspired by the tavern—he sweats vice and reeks crapulousness; one would not give him a dog to look after; no one would willingly exchange two words with him; but everyone stops to listen to him! Yes, the majority have a mocking smile on their lips; but that is because they are slightly ashamed; that mockery is a kind of modesty. They excuse themselves: "It's true that it's a waste of time, but . . ." with simplicity: "one gets bored, and these people are sometimes funny," or with pretention: "It's necessary to see how far stupidity in accompany with mendacity can go."

False excuses. The true reason is both higher and lower. It is the Imagination that the street-hawker addresses, and that is what responds. The predator of centimes hides under exteriors that intrigue. That merchant is a physician and an artist, a sorcerer and a trickster, a bad joker who makes people laugh anyway. He doesn't believe in anything; he teases God and the Devil alike, and yet the echo of the oldest superstitions vibrates with his hoarse voice in the souls of the passers-by; he is Merlin and Voltaire, reviewed by Gavroche.[1] He is the mud of centuries and pavements. He is Art and Science, Philosophy and History, Tradition and also the Fronde in the style of the streets. He is the Street, fantastic and banal, filthy and sublime; the future and the past confront one another there, battle there and are confounded in the deafening hubbub of contradiction in which affirmation denies, faith is atheistic, sincerity is cunning, skill is

---

1 Gavroche, the street-urchin featured in Victor Hugo's *Les Misérables*, became an archetypal figure in the Parisian imagination.

ingenuousness, ignorance knows, love detests, wisdom is folly, praise insults and words strive to contradict their meaning, where simplicity is travesty, everything glistens except gold, where everyone lies to everyone without anyone being deceived—that phantasmagoria, in sum, illusory and real, which we call the Present.

Having finished his patter, the street-hawker causes to spring forth from his depths a gray cardboard box pierced with little holes. He lifts it overhead at first, with a mystical and hesitant gesture, in order to enable everyone to admire it; then, abruptly, he crouches down and, with a thousand precautions, he opens his box, in which we see agitating in all directions twenty minuscule white swallows.

Interest is at a peak. All faces lean forward curiously, the question shining in all eyes.

"What are they?"

Simple pieces of light paper, rather cleverly cut into the conventional—or "synthetic"—form of a swallow when it cleaves through the air, half-folding its wings, in the skies of paintings.

The merchant of impossible things causes his winged merchandise to slide from his box on to the pavement, and immediately the little birds with quivering wings start wandering this way and that, moved by invisible springs, or perhaps by the breath of that absurd God.

And *he*, enjoying the general emotion, says: "Mesdames et Messieurs, as you see, they really are living swallows . . . no springs to rewind! If they don't have the stature of conscripts, that's because they come from the land of the Pygmies, where the men, and even the ladies, are no bigger than my hand. But such as you see them, my little beasties are well constituted, and they have what it takes to make people laugh and amuse them, adults as well as good little children, without doing anyone any harm and without spending a lot of money! Come on, let's see, who wants one? For ten centimes, two sous, the harbinger of spring!"

Several hands reach out, offering and requesting, and the hawker has already wrapped and tied up two or three swallows, while keeping an eye open and using the toe of his shoe to bring his fugitive boarders back into an ideal circle that they must not cross, when disaster strikes.

The wind, which has already been threatening for a few moments, suddenly rises violently; it blows over the frail swallows, flipping them all over at a stroke—and in the circle where I have placed my character, there is an enormous burst of laughter.

Prisoners, beating the air with vain gesticulations of their little black feet, are flies! The improbable birds were flies stuck with light paper wings.

And the crowd, the unjust crowd, curious a little while ago, hooked and desirous, now boos the ingenious merchant of flies, who, indifferent to that rapid aftermath of glory, is following his fortune, scattered in the wind, with a melancholy gaze.

And I believe that flies are Dutch in Holland, Turkish in Turkey and Chinese in China.

# OTHER MUSIC

RAIN with a sheen of sunlight, one of those jovial showers of March, the month of meteorological fantasies, which trifle with us, embellished by squalls, nostalgias of winter in promises of summer, many a time before good weather is definitively installed—April fool!

Paris likes those moist caprices, already lukewarm, which announce the Spring, and nothing is more curiously pretty than the smiles of Parisiennes—those of the proletariat, especially the young—trotting along in the bright downpour, without a hat or an umbrella, when they shake the droplets of water pearling in their hair from their head and shoulders, with a swift movement, on to the fringes of their bodices . . .

Very young, both about twenty, with their noses in the air, their eyelids amused by the light whiplash of the rain, the girls passed by, singing a song that was rather stupid but cheerful:

> *Rain here, make a bog*
> *It's a party for the frog . . .*

The street smiled at them, and maliciously, bravely stamping their feet in puddles in accordance with the requirements of the rhythm, they splash the passers-by. No one thinks of getting annoyed, so graciously and innocently cheerful were the blonde, fresh, insouciant couple, the very soul of that pleasant rain.

*Rain here, make a bog . . .*

An old monsieur, comfortably dressed, had stopped, under his vast umbrella, watching them coming from a distance. They did not notice him until they were ten feet away; but they suddenly fell silent.

*It's a party for . . .*

The old man had the scrupulous correctness, the dignified and austere physiognomy, of respectable, rented vice that dissimulates. But the blinking of his red-lidded eyes, the irregular palpitation of his nostrils, and the fleshy slackness of his lips confessed it.

Suddenly serious, as if the future had suddenly opened up underfoot—alas!—they went past, the little ones, shivering, they went past the stationary man, whose eyes alone shifted.

And they only resumed their song, now saddened, a few paces further on;

*Rain here, make a bog . . .*

## COMPLIMENTS

"HOW happy one must be if one is beautiful!" she sighed, with a smile, glancing at me,
I remained silent, motionless and impassive.
Everyone followed the gaze of the mistress of the house, and I thus became, for having not said anything, the unique object of general attention.

I was slightly troubled by that, at first, because I could read clearly in all eyes that people were criticizing my silence. In fact, the latest arrival in the drawing room, I had just been introduced thereinto, and save for a few "Bonjour Madames" and a few banalities respectfully and barely articulated, I had not yet shown the color of my voice. As a poet, however, I was only tolerated in that worldly milieu on condition of paying for admission with eloquence, and that interjection of the Lady, a direct invitation to lyricism, reminded me, gently but not without authority, of my professional and social duties.

I had a very keen sense of my impoliteness, and I felt, deep down, entirely of the same opinion as all the people gathered in the drawing room. For nothing would have been easier for me—would it not?—than to string together a madrigal immediately, as was being requested of me. For want of imagination, the slightest effort of memory would suffice. One knows one's classics, damn it!

But I continued to remain silent, now with intoxication and sensuality.

Think of it! It was the first time in my life that I had found myself thinking *exactly the same as everyone else!* That situation had for me the unmatchable charm of novelty, and I savored it like a gourmet.

What! Here's a poet who can't find the gracious word of which a lovely woman is in quest! Is that conceivable?

"No, Monsieur," and "Assuredly not, Madame!" I would have liked to respond to each of those individuals who, from the edge of their chairs or the depths of their armchairs, were peppering me with gazes charged with scorn. And I also wanted to say: "Be certain that I am looking at myself at this moment exactly as you are looking at me; there are not two possible opinions about my conduct, and it's yours that I profess."

Oh, how content I was! *So I'm not*, I said to myself, *the antisocial being or "social monster" that everyone believes! There's a theme of worldly civility on which I feel or think like these various paragons of dandyism . . .*

I had so much pleasure that I even feared not being able to help bursting into laughter, which would have compromised my worldly orthodoxy in my own eyes. I therefore stood up, in the great silence that was embarrassing everyone, it seemed, except me. I bowed very deeply to the mistress of the place, made a smiling general salute all round, and went to get my cane and overcoat from the vestry.

"Come on," I murmured, about an hour later, as I closed my door behind me, "I was definitely wrong to worry when I asked myself, before: 'Have I or have I not the sentiment of propriety, of usages—of etiquette, in a word?' That sentiment, I can see very well that I possess, and the proof has been provided."

# ON THE ROAD, AT NIGHT

THE END of an evening in late autumn, moonlit. The deserted road, illuminated; the moon triumphant, and no stars. The thin shadow of trees, already semi-denuded, in the background; the faint lights of villages, glimmers that the electric light of the moon made golden, and which were going out one by one, abruptly. Everything had fallen silent, except for the rare and sinister cry of a guard dog or the threat of a nocturnal raptor.

The young soldier, on the road, in the night, was going rapidly, returning belatedly from some leave, still a considerable distance from the town and the barracks; the young soldier was going rapidly, and the time seemed long to him. Truly, he would never have thought that he would look forward so much to quarters, orders, the hard obligatory bed, confinement and the company!

Also, how many stories there were in the nearby village where he had just spent his day of liberty, how many unusual stories, about the road that he was now taking! A murder had been committed there, a few days ago, in strange and tragic circumstances, and the murderer was still unknown, as well as his accomplices. By virtue of some unknown incuriosity, as well, the place had no surveillance, and robbery, it was said, was exercised there with an admirable independence.

The young soldier recovered all those warnings from his memory, and, brave as he was, he would have preferred the hour to be less advanced . . .

A shadow in movement, out there, ahead of him, enormous, but human even so. By what fantasy, at this hour, was a passer-by walking along this road, magnified, bizarre and as if waiting for some random prey? But what could the young soldier have to fear? His pocket was light, and he obtained some confidence from the bayonet that was beating his thigh. However, the exaggerated stature of the stroller . . . And not hiding, more to be feared, it seemed, than if he had allowed himself to be divined crouching at some bend, ready to pounce . . . Perhaps the sentinel of a troop . . .

But what? The young soldier kept on marching, and, to give himself heart, he started singing a refrain of the region:

> Up there on the mountain
> I heard someone weeping;
> It's the voice of my mistress,
> And I'm going to console her.

At the sound of the voice the stroller turned his head, stopped, interrogated the area, and then, informed, resumed his coming and going. At closer range, the young soldier distinguished a man of tall stature, to be sure, but not as immeasurable as the moonlight had implied at a distance. His costume was that of a horse-dealer on the day of a fair; in his hand was the traditional staff with a leather pommel studded with golden nails.

> Speak, lovely shepherdess,
> What have you to bemoan?
> "If I'm weeping, it's in tenderness,
> For having loved you too much . . ."

Closer still, and then very close, the probable horse-dealer stopped again in order to let the troubadour pass, who looked as he passed at the stout trafficker in living meat, himself a heap of rude flesh. He grunted, but remained motionless, and the young soldier was annoyed with himself for his vain emotion.

The moon was casting its last light, as pale as white nuances coming from the pre-dawn twilight, and the shiver of morning, awakening the crowing of cocks, and crisping the grass on the roadside, invited the marcher to hurry.

Still ashamed of allowing himself to be deceived by the moon's lies, he went lightly, inaccessible henceforth, he believed, to vain emotions.

He went on . . .

What's that, out there, far away, as far as the gaze can reach? What is it? Three large motionless forms seem to be watching the road. They have just suddenly revealed themselves at a turning. Perhaps they're moving, but one can't be sure. Perhaps they're moving, unless it's the moonlight playing over their white garments.

Certainly, their presence is not one that might be expected. And, after all, what are they doing there, if they're human forms, those three immobile things, so tall and so white?

The trooper halts, intrigued rather than anxious, but disconcerted all the same.

What is there to gain by staying there, however? They don't give the impression of thinking of arguing with some passer-by, the three unknowns out there, standing up in profile on the right-hand side of the road. It will be necessary, sooner or later, to approach them; might as well do it right away.

Hey! That's not appropriate—the legs are a trifle wobbly. Not with fear! Damn the petty claret wine that one can drink for a sou in the nearby village! Let's go! It's necessary to march, and to get it over with, at the double!

> Will you show me the way, up there,
> Will you show me the way . . . ?

The singular, frightening thing is that, in contrast to the first fellow just now, these, as one gets closer to them, seem to grow even taller! Are they two hundred paces away? Now they're giants, evident and impossible! Now the moon is veiled; the sky is blurred with rain-clouds.

Nothing can any longer be made out clearly, but, in order to believe, it's necessary to know, whether those three long white streaks out there are three men, or three beings that are affecting, outside of all plausible proportions, human form.

For the second time, a halt.

The first apprehensions, still vague and arguable, are succeeded by the special constriction of the throat that is so dolorous, and contributes, by physical suffering, to troubling the imagination. What? It's only an illusion, a hallucination; one sometimes dreams without being asleep . . .

The young soldier closes his eyes, and mistrustful of himself, presses them with his hands; we'll see in a moment whether they're still there, the incomprehensible sons of Lot!

For those Unknowns have the enervating particularity that they are affecting the attitudes of statues, certainly out of place, exactly as if men had been surprised by a sudden rain of frost, overwhelming and congealing, which had imposed their eternal presence on the road.

Eternal, yes! The eyelids have reopened and they're still there, the long white streaks that are men . . .

A little cold sweat begins to pearl on the young man's forehead and shoulders. Well, yes, fear! Not precisely of a real, tangible or even possible danger. Three marauders, three assassins that one can see and that it's necessary to confront, that is not above the strength of an armed, vigorous man in control of himself. But the fantastic aspect of the encounter, that dream-like immobility, that is what conceals the truly dangerous character of this.

Those phantoms are like as-yet-mute warnings, on a threshold of infinity, who are doubtless going to proffer redoubtable syllables.

Livid, without being able to repress a tremor of all his limbs, the young soldier continues his march.

The sky is increasingly somber, and prolongs the distance, in a way, as it diminishes in reality. Two hundred paces. A hundred paces.

And whatever awaits out there, on the edge of the road, retains its mystery.

It is no longer a question of singing. The sound of the voice, in moving circumstances, is a strength that one seeks outside oneself, a confession of weakness that retains a hope and protests that one still has the confidence of being able, by natural means, to ward off a natural peril. That isn't the case here. True dangers part the lips without permitting any sound to be exhaled, and it is the moment when the most incredulous would like to be able to pray.

The marcher has made the decision to go on, head bowed, without looking again at the oppressive apparition that was recoiling in front of him. That attitude becomes insupportable to him. Suddenly, an abrupt rage inspires him with an action scarcely deliberated but already resolute, the desire to call out in a loud voice to the taciturn trinity and even to insult them, in order to move them, in order to constrain them to some manifestation that will bring them closer to him, which will simply demonstrates that they are human.

He had already raised his head when a new fear stopped him. Now he distinguished, perpendicular to the three vertical lines, a second line twice interrupted: the three phantoms had opened their arms! And he looked at them, stupefied, as motionless as them . . .

In the distance, the town was beginning to salute the new day. Very distantly, appeals were dying in the shadow. All the fires were extinct and white and gray plumes of smoke were emerging from the first houses.

But he could not hear anything, and could not see anything, except the nightmare that was waiting for him fifty paces away—and those three men with open arms.

Surging forward, fists clenched, lowering his head again, the young soldier, abruptly transported by the fury that is one of the final phases of true fear, raced toward the apparition as rapidly as his legs could carry him.

And, having arrived in front of them, opening his own arms, he fell to his knees.

O blessed surprise! Standing there, in memory of some fine action or in expiation of some crime, was a Calvary: Jesus crucified between the two thieves—white consoling statues that funereal Hecate had betrayed.

Oh, how Christian he was, for that minute, the young soldier! He laughed while weeping, and I believe that he remembered then two or three pious Latin syllables, previously devoid of meaning for him:

*O Crux, Ave!*

# FRANÇOIS-LES-BAS

### I. The Gray Socks

... SICKLY evening, black city, where, nervously, with fists clenched, one goes forth aimlessly, like a lost dog, without a goal and without hope, in all directions, marching back and forth, from here to there, and chewing over memoires . . . cruel evening!

Oh, the solitude!

*With eyes full of resignation, but with the intimate irritation of a dolor that nothing can soothe, I witness that perpetual departure—which ought to interest me more—for a risky voyage, of which who can tell me the outcome? Few ports attract me, none retain me. I will go on, however, still, without a goal and without hope. For I am only smitten with the impossible, and I say* No! *to that which could be. My defeat is a frightful victory. When I have used up the territories where fatherlands are assigned, when I have convinced my footsteps to be wholly without hope and without a goal, I shall enter into the arid realm where the mind alone reigns; then my goods and my evils will not be able to communicate with one another. Then, if it happens that I remember the time when I was counted among the living, I shall see us again—you, now forgotten—two delicate phantoms, and I shall have the delight of regret. Gradually, your visits will become rarer; one day, I shall see you for the last time— and that, I think, will be the moment of imminent madness when triumphant thought will break the frail envelope that separates a living being from the eternal unnamed . . .*

Thus, going home, and then closing the door, François-les-Bas-Gris,[1] duly alone, reasons and unreasons like a character in a tragedy.

The door closed, as I say, he stands with his fists on his hips and his back to the fireplace—the winter fireplace, devoid of a fire!—his gaze addressed to the vague walls and beyond, then rolls his eyes beneath his furrowed brows, with a decided, even grim, almost furious expression. He has just quit his "friends" in "society," where there was a certain mockery of the nocturnal color of his socks. He has made, in that nondescript and gilded drawing room, a very adequate provision of sadness for the entire evening. There was a mixed society, bourgeois and artistic (industry and brasserie). Above all, the comrades of letters, and their perfect ignorance, and their vanities, and their projects, which would be new if the Christian era opened tomorrow, have tested his patience. Ordinarily not much of a talker, unless carried away, he is willingly taken for a confidant, not to say a confessor, by the quickly-contented, contented by a sympathetic nod of the head or a compunctious interjection.

But that evening, François had showed rare benediction and lukewarm absolution. He had even interrupted

---

1 Approximately "Francis Gray Socks."

the confidants with gestures significant of boredom. In the smoke of those heavy souls he was so ill at ease and so out of place that when he got up he had to! And now, with the door closed, standing with his hands on his hips and his back to the fireplace, he meditated . . . No, he would have liked to meditate.

Something was lacking.

Ah! Solitude!

. . . To be a cerebral person, or, at least, to be reputed as such, and to be dying of sentimental dolor! To nourish in oneself a demon whose function is to drag you down into the mud of unhappy tenderness, and only to bear in the features, meanwhile, the marks of the fingernail scratches of the terrible Fiction! To be surrounded by poor souls, hypocritical but nevertheless sincere, who have formed an idea of you, a certain idea, this one! which encloses you in the harsh prison of their opinion without worrying about the undulating truth—of course, since it is human, but harmonic nevertheless, but complicated, intense subtle and tenebrous with all the profundities of being! To witness—all too well-placed, alas!—that poignant and ridiculous two-character drama: your veritable being and the conviction that people would like to form on his subject, my dear, and which it is necessary not to betray, under pain of being flagellated by some ironic smile, admiring besides, and which says to you clearly "Well played!"—and not to be able to weep! Oh, François, my friend in gray socks, have your socks dyed then, since everyone wants them to be blue, and, since you're condemned to it, play a role, my master, and allow yourself to be applauded!

*What would my soul say about that?*

. . . How quickly a smile is wiped away! The corners of the lips turn down, the eyes are extinguished and silence rises like a wall between those who are no longer smiling. And if one thinks about a vengeance or stiffens oneself against baleful thoughts, Night, and the immense eyes of insomnia and the bitter sort of shame of having been that weakling who put on such a show of artificial energy, prostrate the soul in spite of pride and render it inapt to the divine duel of the morning, the duel with Beauty, poet! O poet who, for your condemnation, is not unaware that women, beyond the redoubtable secrets of which they are perhaps the unconscious guardians, have scarcely anything to offer you by a refuge of infidel grace, as illogical as it is dear. Have you not, then, made in the intangible and real world of your soul a spiritual haven where, master and priest, you can order the eternal fête of your contentment?

. . . Something is lacking here.

The night embalmed by the reigning moon, the blue night, the joyful night, and the enchanted land of the joy of things. Everything is soft, suave and distinguished, the air light, the tender plaint of a waterfall, there, nearby, and the trees, not one of which is disheveled, and the villas—deserted, it's true—nested among the rosy bushes, everything is very soft, everything is very distinguished. Fortunately, no living being, not even the rustic inhabitant of a Swiss chalet, not even one of Florian's sheep.[1] Everything is very quietly asleep in this nature of amiable operas, in this chimerical and indolent land in which, and this is your mistake, you would never dream of living.

In fact, what are you looking for here, with your clothes as naïvely gray as your stockings and the chimerical flowers of your hat? Preventer of sleeping in peace, you're scarcely the desired guest of this innocent décor. But you, who find all that quite farcical by virtue of being colorless, you fall on the ground, helpless with laughter, with just enough strength left to slap your thighs, rhythmically, like a puppet with a spring, thus expressing the most untimely hilarity.

Be careful: the moon, which can hear you, has clouded over, and, abruptly, everything saddens around your evil laughter; a gray veil envelops the blue night. The villas are more lost than nested among the rosy bushes. Deserted, we said, those villas: if you look hard, you can now see old faces grimacing at the windows, which are trying to provide echoes to your laughter. Oh, how everything has changed! The air is heavier, the silence harsher. It's dark, except that a desolate light radiates faintly around you, which shows, alas, life. Sad, everything is sad, including your laughter.

Are you content? No! So much the worse for you. Suffer for your work. Look what you're able to make of permissible gaiety! Of a pale and cheerful young woman

---

1 The reference is to "Le Roi et hes deux bergers" [The King and the Two Shepherds] by the fabulist Jean-Pierre Claris de Florian.

you'd make some weeper; is the latter, anyhow, truer than the former? For its necessary not to eternalize the gaping moue of this indolent landscape, this spring that forgot itself on stage, no more is it necessary to admit, even for an instant, that October will be more beautiful than April . . . but then, you can't, and there'll be other springs . . .

※

*I know that, and isn't it for nothing that I told you so?* (And François-les-Bas-Gris sobs, his eyes dry.)
Something is lacking here.

## II. The Pink Socks

To which the person who could henceforth be François-les-Bas-Roses has said: *Yes.*
Yes, something, or someone, is lacking in the evening chamber. Oh, solitude!
How dearly he has fêted her, the pretty imprudent, belatedly arrived! How gaily astonished he is by fears, ignorances, confessions, questions, caprices, laughter and tears, supernaturally devoid of causes! A week, a full week, has been for him the wonderment of every minute.
But finally, it is necessary to render to "genius" its rights, and from then on, François, after that delightful interlude, has perched on the heights again. Come in; look.
By the fireside *she* is sitting, slightly surprised to be forsaken. In the depths of her little heart she detests

the strange concerns that keep François poring over his work-table—dusty after a full week of leave—François, hunched under his lamp, his head in his hands, and who is meditating . . . No, who would like to meditate.

For, whatever he does, the presence of the sulky beauty distracts him, and the frightful flight of chimeras only brushes him now with one wing.

Suddenly, his wife, resolutely quitting the armchair by the fireside, gets up stealthily, approaches. And, divine in her amorous design, with an ample gesture, she allows her loosened clothing to fall at her feet, puts her slender hands over the dreamers eyes and, gently and forcefully, presses against the head aureoled with thoughts her pure and beautiful juvenile cleavage.

Oh, François! What! You have the courage to be annoyed?

He has it, the courage! It's unbelievable.

But she doesn't consider herself defeated; madly and delicately, as if he weren't annoyed, laughing, amorous and light, she chatters, chatters—how inopportunely!

From time to time, with a gesture half-supplicant, half-commanding, François begs for silence. She is reluctant, with an obstinate mutiny, and even if she shuts up for a full minute, her attitude protests.

Now, François would really like to meditate.

In the end, he gets good and angry. His eyes and his gestures become malevolent. He is no longer imploring, he is definitely commanding.

"Will you shut up!"

(Is that a honeymoon speech?)

The poor thing burst into tears. He doesn't care.

Then, with a closed, harsh expression, she draws away slightly in order to consider him, and then shrugs her shoulders; then, quickly getting dressed again, she measures him with a gaze of adieu and—without the madman making a sign to retain her—François' wife goes away.

Good silence, beautiful silence! How good it is, François, to be alone, to meditate. Take advantage of it, my friend; direct yourself toward the highest thoughts, put your elbows on the table again, put your head back in your hands. Eh? What are you doing?

Pure human contradiction! François-les-Bas-Roses has got up; he is striding back and forth; he looks at the door, and then stands still, and then resumes marching, and his face darkens.

"Meditate, then, François!"

He sits down again, he gets up again. He opens the door; he closes it again. With a feverish hand he scatters his precious manuscripts. With a blow of his fist he knocks over his faithful work chair.

"Well! What's the matter with you, François?"

# I KNOW THEM . . .

I KNOW many who have made their decision about things and cleverly extracted a profit from everything—I know many of them. They enjoy life such as it is, without remorse and without disgust.

I know some who retain forever in their eyes the virginal horror of the first gaze—I only know a few of them. Their entire life is just one long echo of their first tears. Far from seeking to return the blows they receive, those resigned individuals, they don't even bandage their wounds.

I know several in whom the fear has turned to anger: bellicose souls, spirits in revolt, hearts adulterated by vengeance. If they write, they write proclamations and challenges, the smoke of combat. They neither accept nor grant mercy. They do not dedicate their pity to anyone. They do not implore forgiveness of anyone. They die without a whimper. I know them . . .

I know one who neither wept nor became irritated, disdainfully. I know one who absented himself from that; but he collected stones and rare flowers in his soul in order to build and decorate the temple, the interior temple that everyone would admire one day—when the frail walls of flesh that presently hide it from the world have fallen—the symphonic temple in which plaints and blasphemies will be resolved into amorous harmonies; for no one will weep any longer then and no one will become irritated any longer. I know one who let people believe that he was in revolt, even though he was resigned, wearing his life like a cloak. I know one who knows the secret of Future Joy.

## A PARTIAL LIST OF SNUGGLY BOOKS

**LÉON BLOY** *The Tarantulas' Parlor and Other Unkind Tales*
**S. HENRY BERTHOUD** *Misanthropic Tales*
**FÉLICIEN CHAMPSAUR** *The Latin Orgy*
**FÉLICIEN CHAMPSAUR** *The Emerald Princess and Other Decadent Fantasies*
**BRENDAN CONNELL** *Metrophilias*
**QUENTIN S. CRISP** *Blue on Blue*
**LADY DILKE** *The Outcast Spirit and Other Stories*
**BERIT ELLINGSEN** *Vessel and Solsvart*
**EDMOND AND JULES DE GONCOURT** *Manette Salomon*
**RHYS HUGHES** *Cloud Farming in Wales*
**JUSTIN ISIS** *Divorce Procedures for the Hairdressers of a Metallic and Inconstant Goddess*
**VICTOR JOLY** *The Unknown Collaborator and Other Legendary Tales*
**BERNARD LAZARE** *The Mirror of Legends*
**JEAN LORRAIN** *Errant Vice*
**JEAN LORRAIN** *Masks in the Tapestry*
**JEAN LORRAIN** *Nightmares of an Ether-Drinker*
**JEAN LORRAIN** *The Soul-Drinker and Other Decadent Fantasies*
**ARTHUR MACHEN** *Ornaments in Jade*
**CAMILLE MAUCLAIR** *The Frail Soul and Other Stories*
**CATULLE MENDÈS** *Bluebirds*
**LUIS DE MIRANDA** *Who Killed the Poet?*
**OCTAVE MIRBEAU** *The Death of Balzac*
**DAMIAN MURPHY** *Daughters of Apostasy*
**KRISTINE ONG MUSLIM** *Butterfly Dream*
**YARROW PAISLEY** *Mendicant City*
**URSULA PFLUG** *Down From*
**JEAN RICHEPIN** *The Bull-Man and the Grasshopper*
**DAVID RIX** *A Suite in Four Windows*
**FREDERICK ROLFE** *An Ossuary of the North Lagoon and Other Stories*
**JASON ROLFE** *An Archive of Human Nonsense*
**BRIAN STABLEFORD** *Spirits of the Vasty Deep*
**BRIAN STABLEFORD (editor)** *Decadence and Symbolism: A Showcase Anthology*
**JANE DE LA VAUDÈRE** *The Demi-Sexes and The Androgynes*
**JANE DE LA VAUDÈRE** *The Double Star and Other Occult Fantasies*
**RENÉE VIVIEN AND HÉLÈNE DE ZUYLEN DE NYEVELT** *Faustina and Other Stories*

CPSIA information can be obtained
at www.ICGtesting.com
Printed in the USA
FSHW010736050219
55480FS